SHELF ICE

SHELF ICE

AARON STANDER

WRITERS & EDITORS
INTERLOCHEN, MICHIGAN

Publisher's Cataloging in Publication Data
Stander, Aaron.
Shelf Ice / Aaron Stander. – Interlochen, Mich.: Writers & Editors, 2010.

ISBN: 978-0-9785732-5-6
1. Murder–Michigan–Fiction. 2. Murder–Investigation–Fiction.

Printed and bound in the United States of America
Cover and interior design by Heather Shaw
Cover photograph Jay Burt—walksoftly.com

FOR BEACHWALKER,
WHO HELPS THIS ALL HAPPEN.

SHELF ICE

1

~~~~~~~~~

It was the cold—the biting, bitter arctic blast that hit him as he left the house and ran toward the waiting car—that finally jolted him fully awake. Twenty minutes before, Ray Elkins, the sheriff of Cedar County in Michigan's rural north, had been in a deep, dreamless sleep when he was jarred into consciousness by a tinny, dissonant ringing from his cell phone. The noise stopped as the line cycled over to voicemail. Ray waited, half awake. Then the ring came again, and he fumbled in the dark to get the device in answer mode. "Hey, Ray," came the voice of Ben Reilly, his second in command. "We've got a possible home invasion in progress. Should I pick you up on the way?"

"Yes," Ray answered, sitting up, his feet touching the cold floor.

"Five minutes or less, dress warm," Ben responded.

"How are the roads?" Ray asked as he settled into the passenger's seat and secured his seatbelt.

"The usual, snow covered, glazed over in places." The lights from the dash gave Ben's face a greenish cast.

"I was half asleep when we talked and only have the gist of what you were telling me. Home invasion, hostages?" Ray asked, looking over at Ben.

"It's sort of unclear. We've got limited info. I hope this isn't a wild goose chase."

"911 call?" asked Ray.

"Indirectly. Molly, she's the new 911 operator, got a text message from a friend, a Brenda Manton. It was something to the effect that, 'Someone here, kicking in door.' Molly called me, read me the message, provided a little background and asked what to do."

"And the background?"

"Manton lives alone, deep in the woods. That's all I know."

"What's the location?" Ray asked.

"Southwest corner of the county. Another mile or two and it would be out of our jurisdiction. I've plugged the address into the GPS."

"You totally trust that thing?"

"I printed a close-up map of the area for that address and had Molly confirm the location. It's on the clipboard between the seats," Ben responded, with a small nod of his head, keeping his eyes glued to the road.

Ray peered over at the blue screen of the GPS, noting that their destination was still 15 miles away. "Anyone on the scene?" he asked.

"No, Brett is north. He's rolling. We'll be there before him. Sue's been called in, but we've got to be way ahead of her. Molly is requesting backup from the State Police."

Ray sat in silence for many minutes as Ben carefully maneuvered the vehicle over the treacherous pavement of the winding, two-lane highway. He was still struggling to get fully awake and wishing he had a cup of coffee. He peered out the window. The blowing snow reflected in the beams of the headlights and the pulsating strobes on the overhead lightbar.

He looked out his side window; the woods and fields were held in an inky darkness by dense cloud cover. An occasional yard light at the side of a house or barn provided a break in the gloom. At a few minutes after three in the morning the road was completely empty of traffic, not even a road commission truck clearing snow and spreading sand or salt.

Wearily, Ray found himself resonating with the bleak winter landscape. There was a time when he'd liked these late-night runs, the tension and adrenalin rush produced by the drama of a situation that required the assistance from or intervention by law enforcement.

But in the months since he had been seriously wounded—an attempt by a murderer to eliminate his pursuer—Ray felt his fervor for police work had lessened. He pushed these thoughts back as he dialed his cell phone.

"Central Dispatch, this is Molly," came the response.

"Molly, Elkins here. Anything more?"

"Nothing. I've been sending a text every few minutes. No response."

"Molly, tell me about this person, I'd like to know what we might be walking into," said Ray.

"She's a longtime friend, going back to when we were in high school. We talk everyday, occasional text messages."

"Does she have a pattern of getting in difficulty?"

"Never."

"Husband, boyfriends?

"Divorce, long ago. And not in a relationship."

"Children?"

"No."

"Work, what does Brenda do?"

"She's an artist. Works out of her home."

"So you can't think of anyone who might...?" Ray pressed.

"That's all I know, Sheriff, sorry."

"Let us know if you hear from her."

"Will do. Please hurry."

"What did you learn?" Ben asked as Ray switched off the phone.

"Nothing useful."

"Well good, now we know exactly what to prepare for," Ben responded with a chuckle. Ben was someone he counted on for his knowledge and skillful leadership. And Ray was constantly buoyed by Ben's cheerful disposition and wry sense of humor.

Ray picked up the clipboard and briefly switched the reading light on and studied the map. "It looks like the road into that house is a seasonal road, half a mile or so off the highway. Must take a lot of plowing to keep that open."

"We're almost there. Less than a mile," Ben said. He slowed as they started around a long, sweeping curve, stopping at a mailbox at the end of a narrow road that disappeared into woods. Ben put a spotlight on the mailbox and then the access road. "Looks passable. Do you want to wait for backup?"

"Let's go in," said Ray.

Ben started down the road, bottoming out occasionally in the deep snow. He rounded a sharp corner and dropped down a steep incline. As they started up the other side, headlights came over the crest of the hill headed in their direction.

"What the hell's this?" asked Ben, hitting the high beams and switching on the siren.

The lights continued rushing toward them, rectangular beams mounted high on the vehicle. Ben put the car in reverse and tried to back out of the path of the oncoming vehicle, only to be quickly lodged against high-banked snow.

Ray saw the towering curved blade of the massive plow bearing down on them. And then felt the concussion from the violent impact—the exploding surround of airbags and the sound of breaking glass and collapsing steel. He became disoriented as the demolished vehicle was tossed on its roof and hurled off the road, out of the way of the plow.

Ray, stunned, hung paralyzed in his seatbelt for seconds listening to the howl of the powerful diesel recede into the background. Then he became aware of the fire, a small yellow flicker in the pitch-black night.

2

~~~~~~~

Ray pushed at the door. It didn't budge. He pulled the handle again, this time driving his shoulder into the door with all his might. The door held fast. He brought his knees up and kicked at the windshield. On his second attempt, he was able to kick the blanket of shards clinging to the plastic laminate free from the side of the deformed frame, opening an escape route.

As he attempted to climb out, Ray found that he was still held by his seatbelt. Freeing himself, he crawled through the opening into the snow. He looked back at Ben, hanging upside down and not moving. Ray ran around to the driver's side of the car and pulled on the door handle. It didn't budge. Flames were starting to shoot up from the engine bay.

Ray pulled his radio from a jacket pocket and toggled the transmit button. "Central, on location. Dispatch ambulance and fire. Injured officer at scene." He waited for a second or two to get a response and went back to work on the door.

With his heavy boots, he kicked at the window, his foot bouncing off several times before his toe punched through and the tempered glass fractured into bits. Ray scooped the glass out and reached in and unlocked the door. Then he started pulling at the door. At first he was only able to pry it open a few inches. Putting his hands low on the window frame, he desperately worked the door open a bit wider. He stepped back for a few seconds and thought about other ways of extracting Ben, then returned to the door, wishing he had a long, steel pry bar.

The fire increased, a pillar of flames rising up from the engine. Ray's actions became more frenzied. Finally, the gap was wide enough that he could put his back against the side of the car and push the door with his feet, forcing it open.

"Ben," he shouted, reaching in and shaking the inanimate body. The intensifying fire at the mangled front of the car pulled his attention away briefly.

"Ben, we've got to get you out of here," Ray yelled. He thrust his way through the remains of the airbags searching for the buckle on Ben's seatbelt. As the belt was released, Ben's body collapsed against the roof of the vehicle's interior, momentarily trapping Ray's arms and upper torso. He freed himself and carefully maneuvered Ben's body so he could pull it out of the vehicle. With his arms under Ben's shoulders, Ray dragged Ben's limp body through the waist deep snow, getting clear of the vehicle just seconds before it was engulfed in flames.

Once Ray moved Ben a safe distance down the road, he began to check him for injuries, the scene now lit by the roaring inferno. With his hands cradling Ben's head, Ray pulled the skull and cervical vertebrae into alignment. He put his ear close to Ben's nose and mouth and listened for breathing. The respiration was shallow and rapid. Then Ray slid his hands into Ben's jacket along his neck searching for the carotid artery. It took a while to find the rapid, weak pulse.

Ray was so intent on checking on Ben's condition that he was startled when Brett Carty rushed to his side.

"What can I do?" asked Brett.

"Get an ambulance in here and bring some blankets."

Brett Carty, the youngest member of the department, was quickly back at Ray's side. They covered Ben's body with blankets, tucking them under his legs and upper torso.

Within minutes the township volunteer fire department and an ambulance arrived. Ray and Brett stayed close as the two EMTs, a young woman and a middle-aged man, carefully placed Ben on a backboard. While the EMTs were securing Ben to the board, three firefighters were killing the remaining flames in the now burned-out hulk of the car with blasts from handheld fire extinguishers. And then they helped the EMTs carry the backboard to the ambulance.

Ray followed them and climbed in, standing off to the side as they cut open Ben's jacket and inserted an IV in his right arm. In a few moments the tubing and bag were attached. One of the EMTs, the young woman, was on the radio to the trauma center as the other one continued to work at Ben's side.

Ray moved forward when Ben opened his eyes. He blinked several times and looked toward Ray, only his eyes moving, his head tightly secured against the board.

"What the hell was that all about?" Ben asked Ray, a weak smile on his face.

"Beats me. Probably an attitude problem," Ray responded. "How are you feeling?"

"Got one hell of a headache and an arm that hurts like...," he rolled his eyes toward his left arm.

Ray looked over at the EMT. The man carefully palpated Ben's left arm, starting at the shoulder and working his way down to the wrist. He looked over at Ray briefly and down at Ben.

"Pain's in here, isn't it?" he said, running his hands over the central part of Ben's upper arm. "We'll get a splint on that, buddy. Have you a lot more comfortable in a few minutes. Then we'll run to the hospital. They're standing around waiting for you."

Ben looked over at Ray. "Will you call Maureen and let her know that I'm okay."

"I'll phone her and send someone to pick her up. Just make sure they don't release you before she gets there." Ray squeezed Ben's fingers and then pushed one of the doors open and gingerly climbed out of the back of the ambulance. He found Sue Lawrence waiting for him. Sue, young and intense, worked with Ray on most of the department's major investigations and did crime scene investigations. Ray looked on Ben and Sue as the core of his leadership team.

"How is Ben?" she asked.

Before responding Ray led Sue down the road, away from the noise of the diesel. "He's got a broken arm and probably a concussion. Who knows what else they'll find."

"Fill me in."

"Ben's car got smashed by a plow coming down the driveway away from the house. He was knocked unconscious and trapped in the wreckage. I had a hell-of-a-time getting him out. We've got to get in there and find out what happened," said Ray, motioning down the road.

"I need to get my jeep out of the way of the ambulance," said Sue.

"I'll call Ben's wife. Pick me up on the way in." As a parting thought, Ray added, "Have central dispatch call for another ambulance. Who knows what we will find when we get in there." He paused for a moment. "Also have them put out a bulletin on the plow. The driver should be considered extremely dangerous."

"What's the description of the vehicle? Pickup truck with plow?"

"No. It's a big truck, like one of our county jobs. Diesel with a big curved plow. Can't tell you anything more. That was all I could see."

Sue disappeared into the swirl of snow, pulsating lights, and throbbing engines. Ray moved up the road, away from the noise, and retrieved his cell phone from an inner pocket. He found Ben's home number, pushed the dialer, and waited uncomfortably for Ben's wife to answer.

3

~~~~~~

Ray's conversation with Ben's wife, Maureen, was short and as reassuring as possible. Fortunately, one of Ben's children was home from college and would drive Maureen to the hospital.

Ray wandered up the road toward the house, passed the burned-out hulk of the police car, the smell of burnt rubber and plastic fouling the crisp winter air. He walked 40 or 50 yards more. Sue brought her Jeep up the road behind him and flashed her high beams.

"Who's behind us?" Ray asked as he climbed into the passenger seat.

"Brett Carty is in the first car. State cop in the second. Young guy, Charles something, didn't get his last name."

They snaked up the road between the high banks of snow, finally rolling into a plowed clearing in front of a small log building. Sue rolled to a stop, leaving room for the other two cars to move to her right and left. She switched on the high beams, clearly illuminating the house. A small, shaggy terrier stood on the porch glaring at them. Smoke curled from the chimney, and light from the brightly lit interior flooded out of the windows and reflected off the snow-covered landscape.

Before starting toward the house, the four officers paused briefly in front of Sue's Jeep. Ray quickly introduced himself and the others to the state trooper, Charles Lagonni.

"Sue and I will go to the front porch, see what we can see through the windows, and enter if it appears safe. I think the assailant has left the area, but let's be cautious. Brett, I want you to cover the rear of the building, and Charles, I want you to provide back up and cover from here. Any questions?"

The three other officers nodded their heads, indicating that they were clear on what to do next. As Ray and Sue approached the porch, the dog took a menacing stance at the front door, the hair on the back of his head standing stiff, his mouth open, and his lips pulled back displaying his teeth. A low growl became a sharp, hostile bark.

"Just what we need," said Ray, looking over at Sue. "What do we do now?"

Sue holstered her weapon and approached the dog, talking in a low, quiet voice. With her right hand she gestured, moving an open hand from shoulder height down toward the ground. The dog, quiet now, attending to her voice and actions, stood for a long moment, peering directly into her eyes then dropped to his haunches. She slowly climbed the three steps to the porch, and approached the dog. Carefully reaching out with a heavily gloved hand, she allowed the dog to sniff at it as she continued talking in a comforting tone. She extended a hand farther, softly touching the muzzle of the frightened animal. Cautiously she brought her left hand forward and began to pet the dog.

As she stroked the dog's head with one hand, she moved to its side, slid her other hand behind his front legs, and cautiously lifted him as she came to her feet. Holding the dog under her arm, she carried it to the state trooper.

"Put him in the back of my car," she said, passing him the dog.

Ray and Sue climbed back onto the porch and peered into the window, cautiously at first, and then leaving the cover and moving to the center of the window where they could get the best view of the interior. After removing their winter gloves, they moved to the door, Ray at the right, Sue at the left, both with guns drawn. Ray turned the handle gingerly and pushed the door open with his foot. From an entrance hall, he carefully surveyed the living room and the adjoining kitchen. Sue followed him.

The room was in disarray—furniture scattered, some toppled—showing that there had been a struggle in a space that otherwise appeared neat and carefully ordered. Sue moved to the right and entered the adjoining kitchen.

"In here, Ray," she called.

Ray carefully walked on the opposite side, peering into a bedroom and bath before he joined Sue in the kitchen. She was kneeling at the side of a body sprawled face down on a white tiled floor. There was a small pool of blood near the head. Sue was carefully checking for a pulse.

"She's alive," Sue said. "Let's get the EMTs in here."

Sue stayed close to the victim while Ray went out to escort the waiting EMTs in. Then they quickly checked the rest of the house as the EMTs, two young women in dark jumpsuits, quickly secured the victim to a backboard and with the help of the volunteer firefighters carried her to the waiting ambulance.

"How is she?" Sue asked one of the EMTs.

"Blunt force trauma to the head and face. We'll know more when we get her to the trauma center."

Ray stayed in the house while Sue retrieved her camera and evidence kit. While she was photographing the scene, Ray went out to talk to Brett Carty and Charles Lagonni. He sent Carty in to observe Sue and provide any assistance that she might need. Then he thanked Lagonni for his help and joined the other two in the house.

"How are you progressing?" Ray asked, standing off to the side.

"I've started the process. I'll come back in daylight and complete the job. Her cell phone seems to be missing. I also want to check the exterior of the house. I'll have Brett stay here and protect the scene until I get back and finish up."

"Weapon?" asked Ray.

"Not yet."

4

R ay waited in the car as Sue gave the dog a brief walk down the
road, away from the scene. Returning to the Jeep, Sue opened
Ray's door and plopped the dog in his lap. Then she marched
around the front of the Jeep, climbed into the driver's seat, and pulled
on her seatbelt with one hand as she started the engine with the other.

"He's a she," she said, as she turned the jeep around and slowly
started down the narrow road. "They get things done without a lot of
ritual."

"I sense there is a message there," Ray observed.

"Not at all," Sue responded. "Just a statement of the facts based on
careful observation."

"What am I supposed to do with him?" asked Ray, petting the dog.

"Her. Hold her. She needs to be comforted. She knows something
is very wrong."

Sue slowed as they approached the burned-out hulk of Ben's Ford.

"My God, it looks like the front of the car was completely crushed
before the fire."

"It was," said Ray.

"It was a good thing that you were here and could pull Ben from the
car." Sue looked over at Ray, "Where's your car?"

"I was riding with Ben. He picked me up on the way," Ray explained.

"You were with Ben? You were in that car?" Sue asked, concern in
her voice.

"Yes, like I said."

"How did I miss that? It never occurred to me. There were so many vehicles by the time I arrived I just assumed.... Are you okay? How did you get out of there?"

"I'll probably be sore later today or tomorrow. We got banged around pretty good when the plow hit us. The airbags popped, and I could feel the pull of the seatbelt."

"How many times did the plow ram you?"

"Just once. He was really on the pedal." Ray explained to Sue how he kicked out the windshield and struggled to free Ben from the car. "He was out cold; must have hit his head, maybe in the initial crash."

"Shouldn't we take you to the hospital and have you checked over? You're still in recovery mode. Getting tossed around like this isn't what the doctor ordered."

"I'm okay. I want to get back to the office and question that new person in dispatch, Maggie whatever her name is."

"It's Molly, not Maggie."

"Molly. What do you know about her?" asked Ray as he fished for his cell phone.

"Not much," said Sue, as she carefully maneuvered down the two-track. "She's been in a few of my yoga classes. She's quiet and very pleasant. Her family has had a summer place up here for generations. I think there was a farm in the family way back."

"What's her last name?" Ray asked, looking at the face of his phone.

"Birchard, that's a maiden name. I think she's been married though."

"What did she do before she started working for us?" Ray asked.

Sue paused at the end of the two-track and waited for a pickup to pass before pulling onto the highway. "I'm not sure exactly. She's an artist of some sort, maybe a potter. And I think she was doing art and working in one of those shops in North Bay. I talked to her after her interview. She told me she had to find something steady, something with health insurance. She's single parenting, got a son, eight or nine. She said she couldn't afford to be an artist anymore. Not in this economy."

"Lots of people up here barely make it, even in the best of times."

They rode in silence for several minutes. Then Ray held up his phone, "Do you have a battery charger for this onboard?"

"Not for that," said Sue. "I've just got the standard issue, not one of those fancy ones."

"Well the fancy phone is out of juice. Would you call dispatch and ask Molly to stick around after her shift? It sounds like she can give us some background on this victim."

As Sue made the call, Ray looked out at the snowy landscape in the gray winter dawn. Taking care not to be observed, he put his right hand into his unzipped jacket and felt along the left side of his chest. He had become aware of a dull ache and was beginning to wonder if he had cracked a rib. *Probably just a bruise*, he thought, unable to pinpoint the source of the pain.

"The weapon, any ideas?" Ray asked, bringing his focus back to the case.

"I wasn't able to get a clear view of her injuries," said Sue. "But I would bet something round and heavy, maybe a piece of pipe or a club. There was a lot of anger there. Whoever did this was intent on killing her. "

"Let's hope she survives and can identify her assailant. I'd like to get him behind bars fast."

A few hours later, Ray was just getting off the phone with the hospital when Sue, carrying the dog under her arm guided Molly into his office. As Ray remembered, she was tall for a woman, at least his height, perhaps taller. Molly had the kind of body Ray's mother would have called "long-waisted." Her blonde hair was pulled into a ponytail, a black velvet ribbon holding it in place. Her bright crimson lipstick contrasted with her delicate complexion. A fleece jacket matching her lipstick covered a chambray button-down shirt. Jeans and worn hiking boots completed her ensemble. *The up north costume*, Ray thought. They settled around the end of the conference table.

Sue started to pour coffee into some heavy, worn mugs. Waving her off, Molly said, "None for me, thanks. I'm coffeed out."

"We need your help," started Ray.

"What's Brenda's condition?" Molly asked.

Ray studied Molly's face as he answered, noting her anxiety. "She's had major trauma to the head. They're trying to stabilize her. Her condition is extremely grave."

"Are they going to operate?" she asked.

"They are still assessing her injuries and conferring with a neuro unit in Grand Rapids. There's a question about whether it would be better to fly her there."

Ray waited, allowing his words to sink in. He watched as Molly's eyes filled with tears. He pulled a box of tissues from his desktop and slid them toward her.

"We need your help, Molly," he said after a few moments. "You need to tell us about Brenda. Do you know anyone who might want to hurt her?"

Molly moved around in her chair, pulling her body out of a slouch. She looked at Ray, then at Sue. "Brenda is my best friend. I've known her since ninth grade."

"Was she in trouble? Did she have any enemies?" Ray asked.

"No, no to both questions. Brenda is a wonderful person. I don't think she has any enemies."

"How about lovers, current or ex?" Sue asked.

Molly was silent for a long moment, and then answered, "I don't think so. She didn't have those kinds of relationships. She didn't pick that kind of men."

"Is she in a relationship now?" Sue asked.

"Not in the romantic way."

"Explain," prodded Sue.

"It's someone who's been in and out of our lives for the last 20 years. We prepped together at Leiston School and were in the same class."

"Does this someone have a name?" asked Ray.

"He wouldn't have done this; he's completely harmless," Molly answered.

"And his name is?" Ray asked.

"Tristan Laird."

"Interesting name," Ray observed. "Where do we find him?"

Molly squirmed; she looked uncomfortable.

"How do we locate him?" Ray asked again, rephrasing his question, his voice firm.

"That's hard to say."

"Why?" asked Ray, annoyance showing in his voice.

"It's just that," started Molly warily, "he lives in lots of places. He's got an old trailer off Dead Stream, out in the swamp. Sometimes he stays there. And he's got a tree house on some family property over near Lake Michigan that he also uses all year. And in the real bad weather he sometimes stays with Brenda for a week or two."

"Like now?" Sue interrupted.

"Yes, but he sort of comes and goes. You never know about Tristan."

"Look Molly, we're trying to find out who did this, and you are being evasive. Do you think Tristan attacked Brenda?"

"I'm sorry, I'm just trying to explain. No, that's not possible. Tristan just isn't right. We all look after him. He was injured in a climbing accident years ago, one of those closed head things. He looks normal and makes sense some of the time, but he's in a different universe. That's what I'm trying to tell you. Sometimes he lives in his trailer, or his tree house, or under a tarp in the deep snow. But the thing you really have to know is that Tristan is harmless. And he's also sort of paranoid. If he thinks you're looking for him, he might disappear into the woods for weeks. He's afraid of police or anyone in authority."

"You're suggesting that he might be camping out in this weather?" asked Sue, incredulously.

"Let me explain. After college, before he was injured, he spent years as an Outward Bound instructor. He is absolutely unfazed by the weather."

"So do you think Tristan was there when Brenda was attacked?" asked Ray.

"I really don't know. I hope not," replied Molly.

"You are going to have to help us find him," said Ray firmly. "How about her family, parents, siblings?"

"Mother lives in Grosse Pointe, she's a lawyer. Her father was a doctor; he died a couple of years ago. She's got two brothers, both are docs. They live in Ann Arbor."

"Molly, I'm going to ask you this question again. Do you know anyone who might want to hurt Brenda?" Ray asked.

"No. I'm at a total loss. She was such a kind, generous, giving person. I can't think of anyone who would want to harm her."

"How was it that you were texting with Brenda in the middle of the night?" asked Ray.

"I know we're not supposed to take personal phone calls, but nothing was happening, not for hours. Brenda is a night owl; she often works most of the night and naps during the day. We were just chatting. I won't get in trouble for this, will I?"

"When you got this message from Brenda, how did you know she wasn't joking?"

"She wouldn't joke about something like this. And I texted her that help was on the way. She knew I was treating this as an emergency."

Ray sat for a moment, lost in thought. "Molly, we are going to have to talk even more. Right now I want you to help Sue with names and phone numbers so we can contact her family. Can you stay and do that?"

"Yes, I'd like to help in any way. I just need to call my mom, she looks after my son when I'm working."

"Call your mother, and then meet Sue in her office. That will give Sue and me a few minutes to go over a few things. Before you go, could you look after Brenda's dog?"

"I'd love to, but my son has allergies."

They waited until Molly had closed the door after her.

"Are you all right?" Sue asked. "You're looking sort of green."

Ray didn't respond to the question. "Molly knows a lot, and she's not giving anything away. We're going to have to sit her down and get her to open up. I think she's a little bit suspicious of us."

Ray started to pull himself out of his chair. Suddenly he felt very unsteady. Sue slid the dog to the floor, grabbed Ray's arm, and guided him back to his seat. The world became fuzzy and slowly slipped away.

5

The next time Ray was fully aware of his surroundings he was being rolled toward the automatic doors of the hospital emergency wing. He was quickly moved into a treatment area, where medics pulled a curtain around his bed, removed his shirt, and applied sensors to his chest. He looked around at the team working over him, men and women in plum scrubs.

"Are you with us?" a middle-aged woman standing at his side asked.

Ray nodded, then said, "Yes."

"Good. Would you give me your full name, age, and date of birth?"

Ray, looking at her, gave her the information. He could see that she was keying his answers on a notebook computer supported on a small, rolling stand.

"My notes from the EMTs say you were having chest pains. Is that correct?"

"Yes."

"Are you having some pain now?" she asked.

"Yes, and I'm feeling dizzy."

"On a scale from 1-10, how would you rate the pain?"

Before he could answer someone else asked, "We're going to start an IV. Is that all right?"

Ray nodded toward the voice, then looked into the gray eyes of the woman who asked about the pain. "Five or six. It's been bothering me for a while. It's just getting worse."

"And you were in some kind of accident earlier?"

Ray nodded.

"When was that?"

"About three this morning."

"And you haven't been checked for injuries earlier, is that correct?"

Ray nodded. Looking straight up into a large, round light, he could see people moving around him. "The person I was with came in by ambulance. His name is Ben Reilly. I'd like to know how he's doing."

"Right now the focus is on you. I want you to chew these baby aspirin. Then we're going to sit you up briefly and have you wash them down with a few sips of water. Okay?"

Ray followed her directions. He chewed a handful of fruit-flavored aspirin. Then two nurses, one on each side, brought him to a partial sitting position. He was given a sip of water from the small paper cup.

"Swallow it all down," the first nurse ordered. Then they brought him back flat on the bed.

Saul Feldman, Ray's internist and close friend, came into view on his right. He felt Saul's hand squeezing his upper arm.

"Aren't you supposed to be having office hours right now?" Ray asked.

"It's my day off. Since I can't play golf in this weather, I thought I would hang around the ER and see who they dragged in."

"He needs to get a life," came a second voice.

Ray focused on the person next to Saul. He recognized Hannah Jeffers, the new cardiologist.

"Now what?" asked Ray.

"We'll do some blood work and tests, keep you under observation, and then see if we can find out what's going on," said Saul. "You were in some kind of accident earlier?"

Ray told him about the encounter with the snowplow.

"And you didn't come in to get checked out?" asked Saul.

"I was feeling fine, and there were things to do. What's going to happen now?"

"Once I go through a few more things here, I'll turn you over to Dr. Jeffers," said Saul. "And when she's through with you, we'll find a few other tortures to put you through."

"I can't be here all day," protested Ray. "I've got things to do."

"Today you're mine," said Saul. "Think of it as a wellness day. You'll probably be spending the night with us, too. So get used to it and relax."

Exhausted and aching, Ray spent the day being rolled around the hospital for one test, then another, including hours in nuclear medicine, having isotopes injected into his bloodstream followed by the imaging of his heart.

Along the way, Saul Feldman found him and provided an update on Ben Reilly's condition. Ben's right arm and lower right leg had been casted, and his skull had been scanned to check for cranial bleeding. He was going to be kept in the hospital for a few days for observation.

In the late afternoon Ray was rolled into the room where he was going to spend the night; all he wanted to do was sleep. But before he could doze off a nurse, a slightly built man who appeared to be in his late 20s or early 30s, came in and began checking his vitals and explaining each step to a young woman who Ray assumed was a student nurse. Before they were finished, Saul Feldman was at his bedside.

"How are you feeling?" Saul asked.

"I'm really tired, but feeling much better. And other than a sigmoidoscopic exam, I think I've had every test this place offers."

"We'll scope you after you've had dinner," laughed Saul. "We saved the best for last. Hey, times are tough. When someone comes in with a valid Blue Cross card, we've got to make the most of it."

"What have you found?" asked Ray.

"I haven't had an opportunity to talk to Dr. Jeffers since they finished with you. I've just looked through the early test results and things look pretty good. Although, there were several comments that you present a pretty battered body, lots of contusions, bruises. I only got bits and pieces of what happened before you were admitted. Would you like to elaborate?"

Ray explained the encounter with the snowplow and told about being rammed and flipped.

"During that time, did you hit any part of the interior?"

"I don't think so, at least not initially. Between the seatbelt and the airbags, I was held fairly securely."

"They do the job," observed Saul, "but you can bang into them hard enough to sustain injuries. So you were hanging upside down before you got out of the car?"

"Yes," said Ray.

"Let me look at your chest," said Saul, pulling off the sheet and, with Ray's help, getting the gown out of the way. As he palpated Ray's chest wall he commented, "Radiology didn't see any broken ribs. But you do have a lot of bruising here. How does this feel?"

"Things are sore, especially on the left side," he answered, showing obvious discomfort as pressure was put on different parts of his rib cage. "How about the fainting?"

"I don't know what to tell you yet. It might be a medical problem that we have yet to diagnose. Or it could be something else, something quite simple. You have been under stress for many hours, I doubt if you had anything to eat or drink. Right?"

"True," said Ray.

"So you were dehydrated, had low blood sugar, and you had been on an adrenaline high. Add to that you probably had very little sleep and you're still recovering from a major trauma. Our bodies can only take so much."

"So, if I'm okay, why do I have to stay the night?"

"I didn't say you were okay, and I want to keep you under observation. We'll talk about getting you out tomorrow if there are no suspicious findings. I'll stop by and see you later this evening. Get some rest. That's an order."

Ray's dinner had arrived and he was picking at some overcooked green beans when Sue Lawrence arrived. He had been carefully avoiding the gelatinous yellow gravy that covered the chicken breast and mashed potatoes.

"What's the big smile for?" he asked.

"It's the look on your face."

"What kind of look?"

"Hard to describe. It's sort of like 'Could they serve this at Guantanamo without the International Red Cross coming in to investigate?'" Sue said playfully. "Wouldn't you rather have some wild caught salmon with a champagne glaze, wild rice with morel mushrooms, and some gently steamed baby vegetables?"

"You're only making it worse," said Ray.

Sue pulled the tray off the table and carried it out of the room. In its place she set a Styrofoam box. She removed the cover to reveal the salmon, rice, and vegetables. She opened a second, smaller container next to the first. "And here's the salad, extra virgin olive oil and a very good balsamic vinegar on the side."

"This is just wonderful. Where did it come from?" Ray asked, disbelief in his voice.

"You think I don't have friends in the food industry?"

Before Ray started on the rice, he said to Sue, "Bring me up to date."

"I suspect you know about Ben's condition?"

Ray nodded affirmatively.

"I stopped to see him for a few minutes on my way in. He's awake and alert and looking forward to going home. His wife is with him."

"And the victim?" asked Ray.

"Once she was stabilized, she was sent to Grand Rapids by helicopter. The last time I checked she was in surgery. Her condition was listed as grave," Sue reported.

"How about the crime scene?" Ray asked. "What did you find?"

"I've got lots of pictures and a good idea of what happened. Other than that, I don't have a lot of evidence, some fingerprints and castings of footprints from the exterior that might be those of the assailant. And no sign of the weapon."

"How about the snowplow?"

"That's something you'll be interested in. When I got back to the office after working the scene, an esteemed member of the county commission was waiting for me."

"Which one?"

"Richard Kinver."

"What's his problem now?"

"Seems someone stole a big truck from the yard of his excavation business during the night. I asked him to describe the truck. He said he bought it used a couple of years ago from the state highway commission, spent a fortune fixing it up. He needed something of that size occasionally to keep some of his winter customers plowed out."

"Any chance that he?..."

"You've got it. One of the reasons he bought the truck was to plow out Brenda Manton. Then he made some joke about her living off the grid back in the woods and how much diesel he had to burn so she could live her green life."

"Did you tell him what happened?" asked Ray.

"No, I didn't want to get into it. The guy is a troglodyte. How does he get elected year after year?"

"So the truck is still missing?" Ray pressed.

"No, it's been found deep in the woods at the end of a seasonal road down in Benzie County. Someone poured gas in the cab and set it ablaze. I checked it out late this afternoon. It's just a burned-out hulk."

"Damn," said Ray. "It looks like we've got someone who's focused on not leaving any evidence."

"How's the salmon?" Sue asked.

"Terrific. Thank you."

"I should've left you to enjoy your meal and then come back to talk business."

"No," said Ray. "We do this all the time. It's the norm."

"And there's one more thing," said Sue. "You had a date tonight."

"Damn, I completely forgot. How did you know?" he probed.

"I guess Sarah left a couple of messages on your voicemail today. When you didn't return her calls, she called your office and asked for your secretary. We women know how to get information. I got the impression from Jan that Sarah will probably be visiting you this evening."

Ray turned his attention to the salad, carefully pouring on the olive oil, then adding part of the small container of vinegar. He looked over at Sue. "How about the dog? Did you turn it over to animal control?"

"No," said Sue. "She's really sweet and very upset. I've been feeding her and walking her. She's in the car. I'd like to look after her until this all gets settled. She has been completely traumatized."

Ray thought about it for a moment. "It's okay with me. We'll just deputize her. Does she have a name?"

"Simone," said Sue. "Molly says the dog is named after Simone de Beauvoir."

"A literary dog," Ray observed. "Thank you for this," he said, gesturing toward the now empty food containers, "I didn't know I was so hungry." He paused, then asked, "Will you pick me up tomorrow morning?"

"Sure, give me a call when you know you're getting out." Sue came back to the side of the bed and patted the back of his hand affectionately. Then she was gone.

6

~~~~~~~

Ray was still sleeping soundly when Sarah James arrived. He woke with a start and pulled her into focus as she stood at the side of his bed. Ray had met Sarah in the early fall when he was investigating the murder of a faculty member at Leiston School, a small private prep school. Over the ensuing months they had started to become a couple.

"How are you?" she asked.

"Okay, I just need a little rest. Sorry about tonight, sorry I didn't...."

"Like you had the opportunity to," she said, smiling and reaching out to touch his arm, moving against the side of the bed. She bent forward and kissed him gently.

"You're a hard man to love, Ray Elkins. I've only known you a few months and twice now I have stood at your bedside and looked at your battered body."

"How was your trip to Chicago?" Ray asked, changing the subject.

"Why are you shifting the subject to me. I was talking about"...

"Sarah, this is anomalous. I've never had anything happen like this before."

"How many times do...."

"It was a random event."

"And when Denton Freeler shot you, that was random. The bullet just fell out of the sky and struck you while you were out kayaking in Lake Michigan?"

Ray remained quiet, letting her question hang, knowing the tone of her voice and her body language reflected her anxiety. "It's been an unusual time," he finally commented.

"It's hard for me to see you hurting," said Sarah, brushing away a tear. A long silence followed. She moved closer to the bed and took his hand.

"Chicago," she finally said, "that's something I need to talk to you about. I had hoped we'd be doing that this evening, over a good dinner and a glass of wine or two. I guess that it can wait."

"Now I'm curious, tell me."

"I don't think this is a good time."

"Please."

"Well, as you know, I flew down for the meeting of the school's board of governors' midyear meeting. My assumption was that things would go on as usual for the second semester as the board searched for a new headmaster. But things have suddenly changed."

"How so?"

"There was concern about not having a strong educational leader, someone with a name and track record, in place as soon as possible. The board is worried about recruitment and retaining students for the next school year. In this economy, all the private schools are battling to hold their enrollments," Sarah paused.

"And?..." Ray prodded.

"Well," she started slowly, "one of the board members, Bob Houghton, had heard about a retired headmaster from a prestigious east coast prep school who had decided to come back into the job market. He had retired a few years ago at fifty-five, only to have his 401(k)s tank. The man has an outstanding record as an education leader and fundraiser. He's been offered a three-year contract, and he's starting now."

"That's probably a good thing, isn't it? It will take some pressure off you."

Sarah squeezed his hand tighter. "Well, he's bringing a couple of people with him, his own management team. That's part of the deal. The board looks on this as a way to strengthen the school and make it more competitive."

"So what does that mean in terms of your position? You've got a contract, don't you?"

"I'm an *at will* employee."

"So you're losing your job?"

"Yes and no."

"I'm confused."

"So am I. This is the hard part. My job at Leiston is going away. I'm being replaced by a member of the new management team. But I've been offered a new position by the board's chair. She is a senior partner in a Chicago law firm, and they're in need of an office manager. And it's one of those offers that's, well, hard not to consider. It's more than three times my salary at Leiston, excellent medical and retirement benefits, and they've offered to rent me an apartment close to the office. And as you know, my Eric is starting law school in the fall. This will give me a way to help support him so he doesn't have a huge debt when he graduates. And they've sweetened the pot by saying that they'll give Eric a summer job while he's in law school."

Ray lay there and absorbed the information. Before he could say anything a young woman came into the room, introduced herself as the night nurse, and wrote her first name, *Kate*, on the white board on the wall facing his bed.

Sarah went to the foot of the bed as the nurse checked his temperature and blood pressure and reminded him to hit the call button if he needed anything. Then she left them alone again.

"What does this mean in terms of us?" Ray asked.

"I don't know," said Sarah, coming to the side of the bed and taking his hand again. "This is all happening so quickly. I didn't want to tell you this way. I was hoping for a quiet evening where I could...well, it will be hard. I'm struggling with this decision." She was silent for several minutes. "I'm sorry I had to break this to you under these conditions. It's just that I have to fly back to Chicago tomorrow, so I needed to explain to you what was going on and why I won't be around for a few days."

"So you've settled on this. You're moving?" Ray asked.

"I can see no other way. You know what the job market is like. What's the possibility that I could find something up here with a decent salary and benefits?"

Ray considered the question, but didn't respond. He knew she was right.

"I should go and let you rest," said Sarah. She bent forward, kissed him gently on the lips, squeezed his hand a final time and pulled away. She moved toward the door, looked back briefly, and rushed out just as Dr. Hannah Jeffers was coming in. They almost collided.

Dr. Jeffers stood at the foot of the bed and motioned toward the door. "*Affaires de coeur?*"

Ray nodded.

"I've been going over all the tests," she said in a very business-like tone. "I can't find anything that might have caused the chest pain. There are no blockages or narrowing." She paused briefly. "That doesn't mean there isn't a cardiac-related problem, but there's nothing we can put our finger on. All of the tests and scans were unremarkable. Saul Feldman suggested other possibilities that might explain your symptoms. He says there's significant tenderness in the chest area, perhaps a cracked rib or soft tissue injury."

"Yes," said Ray.

"Let me check your chest," she said. "Tell me if I'm hurting you."

She helped him pull his gown off and started palpating his chest, moving from his shoulders to the bottom of his rib cage, one hand on each side during the first pass, then carefully running her hands over the left side of his chest, then moving to the right side. She took her time, pushing and prodding, then turned her attention to his abdomen before returning to the left side of his chest.

"You're very tender here," she said.

"How can you tell?"

"I can see it in your face and feel it in the way you stiffen to my touch. And as others have observed, there's bruising, probably some soft-tissue injury, and perhaps some cracked ribs. That said, there are no obvious breaks. I know you're uncomfortable, but everything is exactly where it should be and feeling fairly secure."

"So what's the treatment? Do you tape me or what?"

"We don't tape for cracked ribs anymore. There's a possibility of restricting your breathing and causing pneumonia. I'll check with Dr. Feldman, see what painkiller he would like to start you on."

"Non-narcotic please, I can't tolerate..."

"I've seen that on your history. No problem. An NSAID should provide you with enough relief."

"Can I have my pills and go home?" Ray asked.

"Not a chance," she replied firmly. "The fact that we haven't found a specific cause for your symptoms doesn't mean there isn't a problem. Medicine is an inexact science, you know. We don't have all the answers. I want you here tonight so if something happens, we can get you the needed care immediately."

She helped Ray get back into his gown. "Try to get some sleep, I know that's hard to do in a hospital. I'll check on you in the morning."

Dr. Jeffers started out, stopped, and returned to the side of the bed. "Saul Feldman says you're a kayaker, that you spend lots of time on Lake Michigan."

"Yes," said Ray.

"I need someone to kayak with. I can't find anyone who wants to go out in winter."

"Got a drysuit and a boat?" asked Ray.

"Yes, a custom-made drysuit. I'm too small for the normal women's size. And I have a fiberglass boat with a skeg. Kayaking was a major passion before I went to Iraq. I want to get back into it."

"I haven't been out much lately," said Ray. "I miss it."

"I'll be by in the morning to see how you're doing," she said, heading toward the door.

7

Ray stood in front of a tall oval mirror in his bathroom shaving. He was only a few hours out of the hospital, released mid-morning after a conference with his internist, Saul Feldman. Sue Lawrence had picked him up from the hospital and dropped him at his home so he could bathe and change into fresh clothing. Ray brushed on some warm lather and carefully scraped it off with a razor, one cheek, then the other, under his nose, his chin, and finally long careful strokes from his neck to his chin.

As he wiped away the remaining soap he looked at his upper body. He noted the large bruise on his right shoulder, probably from the seatbelt. There was also a discoloration on his upper arm; he wondered again what he had hit. Maybe he had slammed into the door, perhaps it was just the force of his body against the seatbelt.

Ray rotated to the left and looked at the other side of his upper torso. He could see a large contusion that started at the sternum and extended to the side of his rib cage. Everything was sore: his back, his arms, and his neck. Instead of going into the office, Ray thought about how nice it would be to take a long, hot bath and then climb into bed with the stack of recent *New Yorkers* he hadn't opened yet and spend the day reading.

As he dressed, he reflected on his encounter with Sarah the evening before. He wanted to write about this, to go to his journal and get his feelings on paper. Although he'd only known her a few months, they had quickly developed a comfortable intimacy and rapport. Sarah had become a close friend during a time of pain and recovery. *And now she will be gone*, he thought, feeling suddenly sad and alone. But before he could ponder that much longer, he heard Sue Lawrence announcing her presence with a shout from the entrance. He walked into the kitchen to greet her in slippers, carrying his socks.

"Don't you ever lock your doors?"

"God's country. Nothing bad happens up here," he fired back.

"Do you need coffee?" she asked. "We're hitting the road."

"Yes, coffee, please. My need is desperate. A hospital is a poor place to get any sleep. There were people bothering me all night, making sure I hadn't died on them." As he sat and pulled on his socks, Sue started the coffee, putting water on to boil, grinding the beans, and preparing the French press.

"What's the urgency?" he asked, as he started lacing on a pair of boots.

"There's no urgency," she said, "not now."

Ray waited for her to explain.

"When I got back to the office this morning after dropping you off, I got a call from Central. They had dispatched the Lake Township Fire Department to a house fire. It's Brenda Manton's house. I just talked to the fire chief on my way over here. The building was fully engulfed and starting to collapse when they arrived. They've just been protecting the scene and waiting on us for instructions. I've called the State Police for an arson investigator. Mike Ogden is on his way." Sue paused briefly. "He should get here in a couple of hours, hopefully before the next storm rolls in."

"I've lost track," said Ray. "What's?..."

"An Alberta clipper is on the way. We're looking at a lot of lake-effect snow."

"Who called in the fire?"

"It was a conservation officer. He had spent most of the night looking for a poacher, someone had been reported shining in the area. He noticed a glow on the horizon and went to investigate, found the fire, and called it in."

"You had finished processing the scene?"

"Yes, but I like to know that I can go back a second or a third time."

"The road had been closed off?"

"After we secured the building, I had Brett string police lines around the exterior and put some barriers at the end of the access road."

"You should talk to the man who called this in. See if he saw anything."

"I've arranged to meet him later this afternoon. He's going to stop by the office on his way home." Sue paused for a few moments, "That's the first piece of bad news."

"Okay, give me the rest."

I talked to a doctor at Spectrum about Brenda. He's not optimistic, says there's just too much brain damage. It looks like Brenda is going to die without ever regaining consciousness."

Sue set Ray's travel mug on the table in front of him and carefully filled it.

"Why don't you go out and look at the scene, and I'll go to the office," said Ray. "This whole investigation is spinning out of control. We've got to get some focus before things start getting cold."

"Have you had any breakfast?

"I'll get something later. We'll meet when you get back from the crime scene," Ray said as he started to pull himself out of his chair.

"Stay for a minute," said Sue. "We need to talk."

Ray settled back into his chair.

"I had a conversation with your doctor this morning on my way in."

"Which one?"

"Feldman. He said he would have preferred to keep you hospitalized for a day or two longer for observation, but he knew that was impossible. He doesn't want you to drive, and he directed me to make sure you had regular meals and get some sleep."

"So what's he thinking, you're my keeper?"

"He said he told you the same thing."

"I don't remember the driving bit."

"Ray, I'm not used to you being a grump," Sue paused briefly. "I'm sure we can find something for you to eat here in one of the best-stocked larders in the north. Then we will be on our way."

8

~~~~~~~~

Ray carefully cleaned the large whiteboard in his office, using a spray bottle and special cloth. He moved slowly, thinking more about how to organize the investigation than the task at hand. After his initial pass, he wiped the board a second time, removing all traces of pigment.

He eyed the collection of markers, finally settling on a dark blue. Moving to the top center he penned *Brenda Manton*. Then he moved to the left side of the board and started listing categories of people who might provide information that would lead them to Manton's assailant: friends, family, neighbors, professional contacts, community (yoga, coffee shop, church, organization, medical, hair). After he had finished the list, Ray moved up to friends and wrote Molly Birchard and Tristan Laird.

Moving to the left, he jotted *snowplow* and *scene evidence*.

Sue entered the office, carrying Simone, the terrier, under her left arm, and stood at Ray's side and viewed the board.

"What have we got?" she asked taking in the information.

"An early draft, just a sketch," said Ray. "I'm not sure my brain is really here yet." He looked at the dog, "Are you sure you shouldn't drop her off at animal control?"

"She's no problem. I think that would be one more trauma. Are you okay with my keeping her around until we find a suitable place for her?"

"Sure. We'll make you our K-9 officer."

They settled at the conference table, the dog in Sue's lap.

"What's happening with the press?" Ray asked.

"I put out a brief statement that an area woman had been assaulted in a possible home invasion. I noted that the woman had sustained injuries and had been hospitalized. I also reported that a sheriff's deputy had been injured near the scene and a department vehicle damaged by the likely assailant."

"You didn't give away much."

"We hadn't had a chance to talk about a media strategy. I didn't know what you wanted out there. And at that point I hadn't even confirmed that the victim we removed from the house was Brenda Manton."

"And you have?"

"Yes," said Sue, shifting the dog around on her lap. "Manton's personal physician provided a positive identification before she was transported to Grand Rapids. I also notified the receiving hospital that Manton should be provided extra security. I didn't know whether or not you would be available, so I told the TV reporters that I'd try to give them an update this afternoon, something they could run on the evening news. Do you want to do the interview?"

"No, go ahead. You've done a good job developing your role as the department spokesperson."

"What more should I tell them?"

"I think we disclose the victim's name, that she's been transported to a down-state hospital for treatment, and that we are pursuing a number of leads. And then the usual community appeal, anyone who might have information relevant to this case should contact us immediately. Have them put our phone number, the silent witness number, and our email address on screen. Think that will be enough to keep them satisfied?"

"Yes. They're so lightly staffed these days that there's no one with the extra time to really birddog us for more info."

"How about the paper?"

"Since they laid off their crime reporter in the fall, they just run what we give them."

"It makes our life a bit easier, but long term it's not a good thing. It lets our local politicos muck about without any accountability. And speaking of accountability, we need to start with Richard Kinver."

"Do you want me to get him in here?"

"No, I want to go out to his place. Talk to him and get a list and talk to anyone who had access to the truck. And I'd like to do that this afternoon. I'll call him as soon as we finish."

Ray stood and walked toward the board. "When you worked the scene, what did you get?"

"No smoking gun, but I think I can tell you what probably happened. The assailant kicked in the door. She had locks and deadbolts, and unlike you, she used them. But everything around the door was shattered. It was a clear case of improperly installed locks. All they were doing was catching the trim board. A small woman could have kicked them in. Not that it mattered much. If the assailant had too much trouble with the door, he would have smashed through a window."

"So, do you have a scenario?..."

"I think this all happened really fast. I think the assailant arrived, kicked in the door, and attacked her. I think he probably left her for dead. It went down in just a minute or two."

"So this is what the assailant knew," he said, starting to add categories and notes: *location, victim lived alone*. Ray paused for a minute, poured some more coffee into his mug, and took several long sips, setting the mug back on the table. "Put yourself in the assailant's head. Three in the morning. The woman lives in an isolated spot. No landline, no cable. Her cell is her only contact to the outside. Obviously, this wasn't random. The person knew she was there and alone. It wasn't a stealth attack, they'd have come on skis or snowshoes if they had wanted that."

"And the attacker might not have anticipated that she was awake," said Sue, "or that she was texting when he arrived."

"How could she send the last message that fast?" Ray asked.

"You don't text."

"I've tried. My fingers are too big. All I do is back up and try to fix mistakes."

"Watch a tenth grader. She was probably real fast and connected at the time someone was smashing their way in."

"You didn't find the cell phone?"

"No, but I'll order the records once I establish the carrier."

"The assailant didn't leave the scene right away. What was he doing, was he looking for something?"

"You saw the interior. It didn't seem torn apart except for a scuffle."

"How about a computer?" asked Ray.

"There was a tower and a big display and a large format printer. There was also a lot of high-end digital camera equipment. She probably used those in her artwork."

Ray's cell sounded. He switched it on and Sarah James' face appeared on the screen.

"You need to take a call?" Sue asked, glancing over at the phone.

"I'll get back to them," Ray said. "Maybe the assailant was going through computer files."

"Why would you spend the time; just take it with you or figure out a way to destroy it." Sue paused briefly. "Maybe the TV-CSI guys have convinced the public that everything is recoverable. And he probably didn't think there was any reason to hurry."

"True. Was there a laptop?"

"No. I didn't see one."

"How about a charger for a laptop?"

"Ray, the whole computer issue was something that I was going to come back to. We've never had a crime scene destroyed before. I did photograph everything in detail. Maybe we can find a charger or cord."

Ray's cell phone beeped.

"You've got voicemail," said Sue.

"So when you're texting, you get a beep like that when you get a message?"

"Yes."

"So try this out. The assailant is doing whatever. Then he notices the phone beeping. He looks at the messages, sees something like 'help's on the way.' Suddenly he's in a panic."

"And when you guys come up the road, he's meeting and greeting."

"Yes. So we need to start with the truck and Richard Kinver. He reported it stolen. We need to start with him and then move to anyone who had access to the vehicle. This is not just a plow from anywhere. This is the truck that kept her road open."

"Okay, let's work on developing the rest of the list," suggested Sue.

9

<hr>

Ray was in the passenger seat of Sue's jeep. "Why are you going this way?" he asked.

"How would you go?" she responded.

"Straight down 22, then across."

"Why?"

"That's the way I have always gone," Ray responded.

"My way is faster. Instead of watching my driving, why don't you do something. Don't you have some phone calls to return?"

Ray took the hint. He retrieved his phone from an upper left-hand pocket and opened his voicemail. There was only one message. He listened to Sarah's voice asking how he was. He touched the pointer on the right side of the screen activating a return call, and brought the phone to his ear. After five rings the line switched to voice mail. Ray listened to Sarah's message, and said, "Just returning your call. Will I see you this weekend?" He switched off the display and dropped the phone back into his pocket.

The sun broke through the clouds and reflected off the glistening blanket of snow.

"What's that yellow ball in the sky?" asked Sue, fishing for sunglasses with her right hand.

"It's been awhile," said Ray, squinting at the glare coming off the snow. "Do you know where we're going?"

"The general area, yes, and I've keyed the address into the GPS. I figured when we got close you would guide us in if the lady in the machine got confused. Tell me about Richard Kinver, some history."

"The family has been in the county for decades. I think his great-grandparents were among the early settlers who came in and cleared the land for farming after the lumber had been cut. And if their history is like a history of so many farmers from that time, they grew crops that quickly depleted the fragile soil, things like potatoes. Eventually they learned what crops worked and what didn't. Cherries and apples replaced potatoes. Somehow the Kinvers got into the sand and gravel business. And with time they expanded into trucking, bulldozing, and road building. When I was in high school, they were a very prosperous family. Richard's father and grandfather were into local politics." Ray interrupted his history to give Sue some directions. "You are going to want to make a left, there's a road just beyond that blue mailbox."

"That's not what the GPS is telling me."

"Trust me on this. The machine wants you to stay on main roads. This is faster. You will be turning right again in about a half mile; I think it's the prettiest little piece of road in the county."

"Still prosperous?" Sue asked.

"I don't think so. I've heard that Richard has run the business into the ground." Ray paused, "You're going to need to slow down so we don't miss the turn. It's just up there." He pointed with his right hand.

"Sure we can get through?" Sue asked. "Doesn't look like it's been plowed recently."

"You will be okay. Put it in four-wheel drive."

As they started winding up the road through deep snow and heavy drifts, Ray said, "I always wondered what the glaciers were doing when they formed this area. Look at these wonderful steep hills. It's only a couple of square miles, and there's no other place quite like this in the whole county."

"And it's clearly faster than following the main roads," said Sue as she struggled to control the Jeep on the twisting, deeply rutted, snow-covered road. Just before they intersected with a highway, the landscape started to flatten.

"Turn left, and there will be an entry just ahead on the right."

"That's what the lady is saying," said Sue, talking over the female voice emitted by the GPS.

Sue followed a plowed drive into a large open area, bordered on three sides by hardwood forests. On the fourth side was a huge crater from where sand and gravel had been quarried by the Kinver family for generations.

Sue parked at the side of a rusting pickup in front of a large steel building; the land surrounding the structure was littered with snow-covered carcasses of rusting and derelict equipment: bulldozers, dump trucks, backhoes, loaders, and assorted pickups.

As they climbed out and approached the building she observed, "They don't bury their dead, do they?"

Ray pounded on a steel entry door next to the main overhead door. After knocking a second time, he pushed the door open and yelled, "Anyone here?" as they entered, their eyes struggling to adjust to the dimly lit interior. Eventually a figure emerged from the back of a front loader at the far end of the building.

"Sorry, I didn't hear you," said the elderly man as he approached, wiping the grease from his hands with a soiled rag. "I don't bother to put my hearing aids in when I'm working on these diesels. You're going to have to shout at me."

"Dell, what are you doing here?" asked Ray.

"I gotta be somewhere. You think I died?"

"I thought you had finally retired."

"I did retire after the kids insisted that I sell off the garage. But after the Missus passed, there wasn't nothing to do but look at four walls. Richard asked if I could give him a lift on some of the heavy equipment."

Ray introduced Sue and said, "We actually came by to talk to Richard."

"Ain't seen him yet. S'pose you wanna talk about that plow."

"Yes, as a matter of fact"...

"A real piece of junk. Twenty, twenty-five years ago when it was new that would have been a good rig, big old Oshkosh. High-dollar, too. But Ray, it was just used up."

"Where did it come from?"

"He got it at an auction in Wisconsin, gave ten grand for it. Bragged to me how he stole it. Hell, it might be worth a thousand in scrap. Tires are bald, most of the hydraulics are gone, tranny is shot, and the engine don't have much left."

"How did he get it home?" Ray asked.

Dell just chuckled.

"Did you hear my question?"

"I still got a license. You wanna see it?"

"I'm sure you do, Dell."

"Yeah, I drove that piece of shit from central Wisconsin, across the U.P. and down to here. 'Cept for the bridge, and I came across that round four in the morning to be sure there wasn't anyone around, I stayed on secondary roads, didn't want no hassles."

"So I imagine you had a lot of repair work on the truck to get it in shape. I know how much you like to put things in perfect working order."

"Yeah, I do. But hell, Ray, Richard is the cheapest SOB I've ever known. I did fix a lot of stuff. Got all the lights working. The wiring harness was rotted, and I had to wire around it to get juice to some of the lights. The air brakes had to be sorted, most of the lines replaced. Engine all but worn out, but I did get it runnin' as good as it's gonna run. But it was all done with spit and bailing wire. Cannibalized what I could from things around here. Most else was used parts, didn't spend much. But I wasn't going to drive that piece of shit if I didn't think it was safe and legal."

"Drive? I thought you were doing mechanical work."

"I was. But Richard doesn't know how to handle that truck, doesn't like to fuss with the hydraulics. And he was only using it on a couple of jobs. Just those long access roads."

"Why this truck? I don't understand."

"Remember how much snow we had last winter? Richard uses a pickup for plowing. And that works okay for most customers. But that Manton woman and one other couple that had a place way off the road, after awhile big banks build up and the plow can't throw the snow over. Before the winter was over, Richard had to go in with an end loader and clean things out so he could get his plow through. He was only charging them 'bout fifty bucks an hour for the loader, but it took lots of time and the customers weren't happy. That's where he got the idea of getting a really big unit."

"So who's working for Richard now?"

"It's just the two of us. Ain't got no construction work this winter. He does the regular plowing, and I keep things running and drive the big truck. He laid everyone else off more than a year ago. Ronnie Toole was the last to go. I think he moved to Florida with his girlfriend."

"The big truck, the Oshkosh. When did it go missing?"

"The other morning. I came in 'bout five-thirty. Thought I'd take care of those roads 'fore there was much traffic. Truck was gone. Thought Richard musta taken it, which didn't quite make sense, 'cause he told me he'd be down in Lansing for a meeting, but you never know about him. And it looked like maybe he took it."

"How's that?" asked Ray.

"Well, I had it plugged in, a block heater, only way you could start that old engine in cold weather. Truck was driven away without unplugging it. Extension cord was snapped, fuse blown. It just looked like something Richard would do, so I didn't think anything about it 'til he showed up and asked where the truck was."

"When did Richard show up?"

Dell considered the question for a long moment. "Can't rightly say. Late morning, afternoon. Something like that."

"How about an ignition key?" Sue asked.

"Key," Dell chuckled. "We never got one. It was just jury-rigged, lots of loose wiring. I put in a new ignition switch and starter button. Hell, no one comes in here. It's never been a problem."

"So you plowed the road into Brenda Manton's. When were you last in there?" Ray asked.

"I think it was the weekend, maybe Monday. Ray, I just lose track."

"Did you know her?" asked Sue.

"Nice lady. She invited me in a couple of times. Give me some coffee. I talked to the dog. Don't know why anyone would want to hurt her."

"Was there ever anyone else there?"

"No, just her and the dog. She parked that little Honda SUV near the front. I had to clear that whole area out so I could get the rig turned around."

"Dell, if I didn't know about trucks, could I have started that truck and driven it?"

Dell reflected on the question. "You wouldn't need to be no Wernher von Braun, it was just a big, old truck. And that 9-speed tranny is a bitch, but if you had any mechanical sense, you might figure it out."

"Any chance Richard took the truck?" Sue asked.

"Never know about Richard. Acted like he didn't."

Ray looked around the shop, "This used to be a thriving business."

"It was. I did lotsa work for Richard's dad and granddad, both good men. Hard workers, lived carefully, they really built something. Didn't take Richard long to go through it all," Dell said with a chuckle. "Big house on the water, living high on the hog. Soon as the house was in default, that cute little wife of his was gone. Rumor has it she took off with some summer person, old guy with big bucks."

Ray heard the sound of a truck door being slammed, then a long column of light appeared as the door was pushed open.

"Sheriff, you're a hard man to find," said Richard Kinver, joining the group. "I'm glad you're here. I need to get this truck thing resolved so I can get the insurance people in here." He turned toward Dell, "Man, you better get hopping on that loader. We're going to really need it now that we don't have the truck."

"Good to see you Ray, and you, Miss," said Dell, as he ambled off toward the far end of the building.

Richard waited until he was out of earshot. "Yeah, Dell is a good old boy, but these days he'd rather talk than work, so I have to keep after him. Like I was saying, I need to get the insurance adjuster involved. I still can't believe that someone stole my truck. I spent a fortune on that rig and a second one having Dell rebuild it. He brought it right back to the original specs. Dell damn near bankrupt me with all the new parts he put in it."

"Who had access to the truck?" asked Ray.

"Just the two of us."

"And who drove it?" asked Sue.

"I only used it on two jobs, long access roads that we were having a hard time keeping plowed with a pickup. I let Dell drive it. It's his baby, and since his wife died he's been down. This truck project has sort of given him something to live for. He's an old family friend; I'm doing what I can to help him out."

"Did you know how to drive that truck?" asked Sue.

"Look, lady, I started driving trucks and heavy equipment as soon as I could reach the pedals—before I had my license, just around the yard here or over in the pit. But, in truth, that was Dell's truck. And I let him do the two jobs. He didn't have to go too far, so he wasn't putting anyone at risk."

"I don't know anything about your business. What's a piece of equipment like that worth?" asked Ray.

Richard looked thoughtful, nodding his head a few times like he was adding numbers. "I don't think Oshkosh makes anything quite like that anymore. They're doing more specialized equipment for airports. But new, something comparable would probably be a couple-hundred grand. That truck may have been old, but after Dell finished with it, it was damn near perfect mechanically. I think maybe fifty or sixty thousand. I'm going to have to get busy and start putting some numbers together for the insurance people."

"Brenda Manton, how did you get that job?" Ray asked.

"I did the excavation work when she was building. Her contractor, Bob Karls, hired me. There was a small, cement-block structure on the site that had to be demolished and removed and the two-track had to be widened enough to get construction equipment and materials in. She was a real pain in the ass because she didn't want any trees cut down or the road improved. Finally Bob just told her he couldn't build the house if he couldn't get a cement truck in."

"So you got to know her?"

"Not really, I let Bob deal with her. Woman like that bothers me, always hanging around watching. But that first winter she got her little SUV royally stuck. So she called wondering if I could plow her out and keep her road open."

"When did you last see Manton?" asked Sue.

"Let me think, sometime in the fall. I stopped by to tell her that we'd be using a new piece of equipment, bigger and noisier, but it would do a better job and wouldn't be damaging any of her precious environment."

"How did that go down?" asked Sue.

"Seemed okay by it. She'd finally figured out what it takes to live in the woods."

"And you hadn't seen her since?"

"No, Sheriff. It's just like I told you. Now if you don't have any more questions, I've got things to do."

"I've got one more question," said Ray. "Where were you on Wednesday night and Thursday morning?"

"What the hell are you thinking?" Kinver answered.

"I just need to know where you were," Ray responded in a flat, even tone.

"I was in Lansing at the workshop for county government people."

"What days?"

"It was all day Wednesday, ended late in the evening. I stayed at the Holiday Inn, came back Thursday morning."

"Who can substantiate this?" Ray asked.

"You can ask Mike McFarland, he was there, too. That is if the word of another county commissioner is good enough," said Kinver. "We are the two senior commissioners, our recommendations have a lot to do with the funding of your department."

"I know the people in this county appreciate your diligence and hard work on their behalf. Thank you for your time." said Ray. "We might need to talk to you again."

"When do I get my truck back?" asked Kinver, his tone remaining hostile.

Ray looked over at Sue and let her answer, "It's evidence in a crime. We're not done with it yet. I'll let you know."

As Sue fought her way down the unplowed road, Ray asked, "Why are you going this way?"

"I heard it was faster," she responded. "What's next?"

"Would you check with Mike McFarland and see if Kinver's alibi holds up?"

"Will do."

"Chat him up a bit before you hit him with the question." Ray looked over at Sue. "What's the smile for?"

"You. You're being so careful not to say what you're thinking. Mc-Farland is such an old skirt chaser, all I've got to do is blink at him a couple times, maybe show him a hint of cleavage, and he'll be falling all over himself trying to help me out. Then what?"

"I'd like to talk to Molly Birchard again. See if we can get her to open up a bit. What do you think?"

"I'd like another shot at Molly, too. I also need some time to carefully look at the crime scene photos. And Ray, I promised Doctor Feldman you'd get some rest. Why don't I run you home."

"I need a couple of hours at the office to do paperwork. I also need to get everything typed up concerning this case."

"We'll get dinner on the way back, and I'll line up Molly for tomorrow morning, after she finishes her shift. And you're going home at nine o'clock."

10

~~~~~~

ay stood at his writing desk, a hot mug of ginger tea sweetened with honey in easy reach. He was reading his last entry from earlier in the week. As he stood there filling a fountain pen with the brown ink he always used, he noted that life had been much simpler only a few days before. In his last entry, he had been rambling on about the weather, a topic he sometimes settled on when he had a need to write but couldn't find a focus. Often writing about the weather or some other mundane topic would prove to be a starting point, inexplicitly leading to something that was worth exploring.

Ray, glancing at the journal he was currently using, a spiral-bound notebook, thought about all the other journals he had filled over the years, the most recent stacked in a near closet, more dated ones stored in boxes in the attic over the garage. *What would happen to these if I suddenly disappeared?* he thought.

Ray had no siblings or close relatives. In his recently revised will he had provided for the liquidation of his assets—the money going to local foundations and the universities he had attended, his books to the local library. But on this late evening standing at his writing desk, physically and emotionally drained from the day's events, it suddenly hit him that he had not arranged for the disposal of his personal possessions, especially his journals. He reflected for a moment on what a reader would find: ramblings on weather, friendship, a particularly good meal or recipe, reflections on romances, narratives on kayaking on Lake Michigan—nothing prurient or salacious or especially interesting to anyone else. One thing that he would never want disclosed were his speculations during the course of criminal investigations. But all of it was personal writing—private, important, Ray's way of capturing and reflecting on his life. It was not for anyone else's eyes.

Ray thought he should ask his friend Marc, and maybe Sue, to be responsible for destroying his journals. Then he would talk to his attorney, Mardi, and have her add something to the will.

He finished filling the pen, wiped the ink from the grip section with a tissue, replaced and tightened the cap on the ink bottle, and returned it to the storage space below the writing surface of the desk. Each step performed slowly and with great care, a ritual, almost a meditation.

Ray started writing, the initial sentences centered on his frustration with the pace of the investigation, how they were just stumbling forward, without focus or a clear organization. There were too many leads to pursue, and he lacked the time and personnel to quickly follow all the strands. Then he thought about the victim, he needed to know more about her so he could begin to speculate on who might want to kill her.

He moved to start a new paragraph, paused and looked back at the word "kill." The incident had started with a home invasion and an assault that had left Brenda Manton gravely injured. *But why didn't the perp finish her off?* he wondered. And then the answer was obvious, he just needed to incapacitate Brenda. At his leisure the perp would search for and remove whatever he was after. Then he'd burn the building down and Brenda would perish in a house fire. They were common enough in homes heated with wood, and that far off the beaten path without neighbors or a nearby road, and in the middle of the night, there would be only ashes by the time anyone happened on the scene. The beeping of the cell phone changed the scenario. Suddenly the perp had to get out of there, probably before he found what he was looking for. And his victim was still alive. Maybe in his panic to get away, he had forgotten about that, forgotten to finish her off.

Ray got it all down and then re-read what he had just written. His fatigue was suddenly gone. He was awake and alert, everything coming into focus. He could see the scene, the interior of the cabin: the bright light from scores of small halogen spots positioned around the interior, the golden glow reflecting off the pine paneling that covered the walls and ceiling, the art—panels of bright wool yarn, some in complex designs, others free-form, and some with colors that were more muted. And then an elaborate array of electronics—computers, cameras, video equipment. And books, shelves of books.

As Ray and Sue had discussed, aside from a few tall kitchen stools near an eating area, probably tossed aside during the assault, everything seemed to be in order. Ray came back to his earlier assumption, whatever the perp was after had to be on the computer. He underlined that thought, paused, and reconsidered what he had just written. *Is this conclusion too easy?* he pondered.

Then the video was running in Ray's head again—the beep of the text message, the perp panicking, rushing from the house, smashing the police car, and finally the destruction of the truck. *Then what?* Ray thought, *the prep had to get out of there*. Then he backed up in his thinking, looking again at the questions surrounding the truck. *Why the truck? There were lots of other ways of getting there: walking, skis, show shoes, snowmobile, car. The first three could be done silently, offering an element of surprise. What had the perp originally planned to do with the truck? Return it?*

Ray pulled a small yellow pad from the shelf under his desk and began making a list of items he wanted to discuss with Sue and perhaps Molly:

Truck—evidence?
Robbery, something else?
Why texting rather than voice?
Any personal connection between Kinver and Manton?

Ray looked at his watch and checked the time. Picking up his phone, he called Sarah's cell. Sarah's voice was instantly on the line, asking the caller to leave a message.

"Ten-thirty our time," said Ray after the tone. "Wonder where you are and when you'll be home?"

He switched off the phone and returned to his journal. Then he looked back at the yellow pad. There were other things swirling in his head, but fatigue was settling in again. He screwed the top back on the pen and returned it and the journal to their place in the desk.

11

Ray awakened to the smell of coffee and kitchen sounds, a dish-washer being emptied, pans being set on the stove. He rolled out of bed, setting his feet on the floor, pushing to his feet, his hand against the firm surface of the mattress. He limped into the bathroom, his leg still stiff and sore at the beginning of the day, a flashback to memories he was trying to escape.

He pulled his robe from a hook on the bathroom door. A vision of Sarah flashed across his brain as he moved toward the kitchen. It was shattered by a couple of sharp barks and an enthusiastic greeting by the terrier, Simone.

"How did you get in? I thought I set the lock," he said, picking up the dog.

"You and your keypad lock," Sue laughed. "It was really hard to figure out the code. When 1-2-3-4 didn't work, I put in your birth year. What can I say, you're the poster child for crime prevention."

"What's this all about?" Ray asked, looking around and seeing that Sue was starting to make breakfast.

"This is about my still being your driver, and I'm supposed to make sure that you have three meals a day, remember? Your doctor didn't want you to drive until next week, until after you saw him again."

"But...."

"But what? All he's got to say is that you've had a stroke, and your license will be suspended."

"But I didn't."

"It's one of the possibilities. Your blacking out is still a medical mystery, and I'm on the side of extreme caution. With Ben out and your health situation up in the air, I'm taking no chances. I don't want to be in charge. You're getting oatmeal for breakfast with a side of prunes."

"What?"

"You heard me. Good for the heart and lots of antioxidants. That's what my grandmother's been doing for years, and she's still going strong at ninety-three." Sue was having fun, there was mirth in her tone and facial expressions.

"And what are you having?" pursued Ray. "I've never seen you eat anything but donuts and coffee, or maybe a Danish and a Diet Coke."

"I'll have what you're having, even if it kills me. Role model and all that stuff."

"I was thinking about the case last night," said Ray, sliding into a chair at the table and setting Simone back on the floor.

"So was I," she responded. "It looks like we both need to get a life. I took a laptop home with photos from the crime scene. I was going to review everything, and then let it perk during the night, see if anything new popped up. But I got home, took a long, hot bath—I needed to get the stink of the fire off me, especially my hair. Then I just crashed. I could barely make it from the tub to the bed. If I hadn't set two alarms I'd still be out."

Sue set two bowls of oatmeal on the table, then brought coffee mugs and the pot. "What do you want on the oatmeal?"

"What does your grandmother do?"

"Lots of butter and maple syrup."

"I'm starting to understand your genetic pool," said Ray. "I'll take some maple syrup. That and the butter are in the fridge."

After Sue settled across the table from him, Ray asked, "What about the prunes?"

"That was a joke. I was trying to totally gross you out. You've got some bananas that are almost too ripe. Want one of those?"

"Sure," Ray. "I was thinking about"…

"Why don't we see if we can have a meal together without talking about work?" Sue interrupted.

"What would we talk about?" Ray asked.

"What do people talk about when they can't think about anything to talk about? How about the weather?"

"That's going to be a long conversation," said Ray. "Snow today, snow tomorrow. The sun will appear again in April. Next topic." He watched as Sue pushed slices of butter in her oatmeal and then cover the surface with syrup.

"Did you make amends with your girlfriend for missing a date?" Sue questioned playfully.

Ray explained Sarah's sudden job change and her impending move to Chicago. His telling someone else about Sarah suddenly leaving made it more real. They ate in silence for several minutes.

Finally Ray said, "So we'll start with Molly, and then we'll be able to spend time reviewing where we are and planning on what to do next."

"The morning, Ray, only the morning. Then I'm bringing you back here and you're taking the rest of the weekend off. You're to relax and take it easy."

12

Ray looked at Molly closely as she slid into a chair across from him in his office. This was his third contact with her. He had met her briefly during the hiring process, and he and Sue had questioned her the morning after the assault on Brenda Manton. Now he looked at Molly again with fresh eyes, and while it had been only three days since their first extended conversation, he noticed things he hadn't seen on their first encounter. He wondered if he had been less than fully cognizant of everything that happened after the jarring collision with the plow. Perhaps he had been able to concentrate on the main events without being sensitive to the nuances.

He carefully observed Molly as she poured a mug of coffee and added milk and sugar. She had the worn look of someone just coming off a night shift—her blouse less than crisp, her makeup in need of touching up. There was also a hint of stale cigarette smoke. Since the entire county complex became a smoke-free zone, the smokers had regressed to high-school like behaviors—smoking in their cars or in a wooded area at the far corner of the main parking area and so far no one had pressed for rigid enforcement of the ban.

"You're in contact with Brenda Manton's family?"

"Yes. I drove down to Grand Rapids on Thursday, and I'm going back today as soon as I get a couple of hours of sleep. I had a long conversation with one of her brothers last evening." Her eyes flooded, and she wiped them with her hands. "You know what's happening?" she asked.

"Just reports on her condition, reports that were less than optimistic. Do you want to fill me in?"

Molly pulled several tissues from a box on the table, blotting tears again and blowing her nose. "They're going to pull her off the machines in a day or two. I guess they've been making whatever type of arrangement you have to do for that kind of stuff. Her brother Jeff, he's the oldest, explained all that to me last night."

"You told me that both brothers were physicians?" Ray asked, checking on his memory of his first conversation with Molly.

"Yes, Jeff is a surgeon and Robert is an internist. Jeff is also a medical ethicist; he did some kind of special degree or program after his residency. He explained the situation to me last night, all the medical stuff and all the other considerations. It was logical and made sense, and the thing about how other people will be able to have better lives because of the organs they're able to harvest. That's the term he used, harvest. Weird."

Molly sipped some coffee. Ray sensed that she was struggling to keep her grief in control. "It all makes sense. Brenda's no longer there. Just turn off the fucking machine...." Molly collapsed in tears.

Sue, who had been sitting silently at the table up to this point asked, "Molly, can I get you anything, water?"

"I just need a few minutes." More tears followed until Molly was able to regain control. "This wasn't real in the beginning." She paused, "Brenda was going to get better. Come home. Everything was going to be fine. That's what I had convinced myself of. Now none of that is going to happen. She's gone, her house is gone, the person that I've been closest to over lots of years, gone."

"Wednesday night," started Ray, trying to move the interview forward, "why were you texting? Why weren't you having a conversation? I can't imagine much was going on in dispatch at that time of morning."

"You're right. Nothing was going on. Brenda had no landline. You probably know that. It was just the cell, and the coverage down in her area is lousy, the way it's tucked back in those little hills. If Brenda walked halfway down her road to the highway, she could have a conversation, but in her house the cell phone didn't work too well, some days not at all, like the weather or clouds did something. But texting always seemed to work. So we'd stay in contact that way."

"Molly, we've talked about this briefly, but tell me again. Why was Brenda up at that time of the morning? What was going on?"

"She was working feverishly. I remember her saying, 'I'm on a roll.' She had a major show coming up in the late spring at one of the universities down state, and she was working feverishly to get things done. Brenda said her art was going in a whole new direction.

"Sheriff, what you have to understand is that Brenda was a workaholic. When she was working on something, nights and days didn't matter. She'd work. When she was tired, she'd sleep. When she was hungry, she'd eat. But the focus was always on the work. And when a project was done, she'd take time off and life would go back to normal for a while. After a few weeks or months she'd start getting antsy. She needed to focus, she needed to be productive, she needed to do art."

"You've talked about your friendship. Did you spend time together when she was in one of these intensive work phases?" asked Sue.

"We talked every day. I'd visit three or four times a week, usually bringing whatever groceries she needed. When she had completed a project, we'd spend more time together. She described her life as having two phases, *in cave* and *out of cave*. When she was working, she was *in cave*. She was absolutely driven when she was working on a project. She didn't socialize or do anything else until she was done."

"So you were a close friend of Brenda's. Who were her other close friends?" asked Sue.

"We were more than just close friends," said Molly. "We have been best friends since ninth grade. I think we were more like sisters."

"I understand," said Sue. "But Brenda did have other friends, perhaps not as close as the two of you."

"I told you about Tristan Laird."

"Yes. Have you been in touch with him in the last few days?"

"He doesn't have a phone or anything. I did go looking for him yesterday. The road into his trailer is blocked with snow, and I didn't have the energy to try to hike in."

"So you haven't talked to him?"

"No."

"Do you think he knows what's happened to Brenda?"

"Hard to say. He doesn't have any electronic stuff, not even a radio. Like I think I told you, he's in his own universe. But he does have a sense of things."

"If Tristan found Brenda's house destroyed, what would he do?" Ray questioned.

"Think about what a normal person would do, and that won't be it. My guess is that he would just disappear for a while. He's really paranoid. Eventually he'd get his fear under control and try to figure out what happened."

"We need your help in finding him so we can talk to him," said Sue.

"You don't suspect?..."

"We don't suspect anything. We need to talk to everyone who knew Brenda. We're at an early stage in this investigation. We're just beginning to collect information. We're gathering pieces of a puzzle that we hope will lead us to Brenda's assailant," Ray said, speaking slowly, stressing the message of each sentence. "We need you to take a map and pinpoint places where we might find Tristan."

"What I'm telling you is that it won't be easy," Molly responded. "Like I said, he's got this trailer he uses, but I didn't see any signs that he was there. And if he's spooked, there's no telling where he might be. Sometimes he sleeps in a canoe that he ties up in a remote spot on one of the streams like the Betsie or the Platte. And this time of year he likes to spend time out on the shelf ice. If the lake is calm, he will paddle out in a kayak and find an ice cave to sleep in. He says he can hear voices in the wind and waves."

Ray was moving his head from side to side. "That would be so dangerous, given how fast the weather changes."

"He's had some close calls, Tristan has. He laughs about them." Molly paused briefly, "And, yes, I will mark out a map for you, but I'm not sure how much help it will be. I don't know many of his secret places."

"Tell us about other friends," pressed Sue.

"Brenda had lots of friends, but we were the close friends, Tristan and me. Work came first, socializing came later. That said, she was very active in the arts community here and across the state."

"Let's talk about people around here, anyone she might be in contact with on a regular basis?"

Molly took a few moments to reflect on the question before responding. "Well, probably Elise Lovell. That's the woman she's been buying most of her yarn from recently. There was a lot of back and forth between them, you know. Brenda was always looking for special colors and textures, and Elise was willing to experiment and produce lots of samples until Brenda found just the right thing."

"How often would they have had contact?"

"Just guessing, I don't know for sure, but probably once a week or something like that."

"Are there other people in the community that Brenda had contact with?"

"What are you looking for?"

"Molly, we're looking for motive. Why was she attacked? What was going on in her life that prompted this violence? People often share things with those they come in contact with. They might talk to a hairdresser, or physician, minister, perhaps someone they do yoga with. See where I'm going? We're looking for the bits and pieces, so we can begin to connect the dots."

"She got her hair cut by the guys at the Third Wave, but not often. And she did a lot of yoga classes, but that was years ago. Recently she's just been using DVDs. As far as religion, she didn't go to church."

"Love relationships?" asked Sue.

"Not now, not recently."

"How about a bad breakup in the past?"

"No."

"She owe anyone money, or was anyone in her debt?"

"No. She was self-sustaining, and I don't think anyone owed her."

"Family problems?"

"No. I wouldn't say she was close to her family, but they all seem to like and respect each other."

"How about Richard Kinver?"

"Kinver, the creep. Brenda told me he'd come sniffing around like he was wanting to offer some kind of trade-out in exchange for plowing service."

"What are you suggesting?" asked Ray.

"You know what I'm suggesting," Molly replied. "But I think he finally got the message."

"Did she ever feel threatened by Kinver?"

"No, just irritated," She paused briefly, "Sheriff, I'm exhausted. I need some sleep. Then I have to get on the road. Can I go now?"

"Yes. You know what we're looking for?"

"Yes."

"What do you think?" asked Ray, turning to Sue as the door closed.

"Just like our first conversation, she's not giving much. We need to find out why." "What's next?"

"I'm going to drop you home. And then I'm going to run down to Grand Rapids, too. See if I can learn anything more from her family. And don't even ask. You're not going."

13

~~~~~~

Ray was irritated at being dropped off to rest while Sue was going to Grand Rapids to continue the investigation. Distracted, he rattled through the refrigerator looking for something to eat.

Standing at the chopping block next to the stove, he cut two slices from a loaf of peasant bread. Ray poured some olive oil into the pan, adding one slice of bread. Then he added slabs of a local raclette cheese and topped it with the second piece of bread. He carefully tended to the sandwich, turning it often to toast it perfectly on both sides.

Settling at the kitchen table, Ray turned his attention to an article in the *New Yorker*, his lunch beginning to cool. The sound of a slamming car door was followed by a vigorous knock at his front entrance. Ray waited, accustomed to his friends just pushing the door open and walking in. With the second round of knocking, Ray went to the door.

Hannah Jeffers confronted him; he could see a yellow and white kayak strapped to the top of a Subaru wagon on the drive.

"You busy this afternoon?" Jeffers asked, sliding past him into the great room. "Looks like you're having lunch."

"Just about. Do you want a cheese sandwich?" Ray asked pointing to the one on his plate.

"That's way too big. How about half?"

"You got a deal. It was more than I should eat," he said, getting a second plate. "Want an apple? I've got some Honey Crisps."

Hannah nodded to the affirmative. "I just came by to ask you if you would go kayaking with me on Lake Michigan. I wasn't expecting to get fed."

"How did you find me?" Ray asked, sitting at the table again.

"Real hard, Google, then Google Maps. You're on my way to the big lake."

"So according to you medical types I shouldn't drive, but you think that I'm competent to kayak?"

"Can't drive? I don't understand," said Jeffers.

Ray explained.

"That's your internist, Feldman. I never said anything about a possible stroke. Saul is a lovely man, but he's overly cautious. Is there the possibility that you had a stroke-like episode? Yes, but a stroke, extremely remote. He was probably trying to find a way to get you to slow down. And from his point of view, that's good medicine."

"So I'm clear to paddle?" asked Ray, knowing that he was still sore, but that he would happily endure some pain to get on the big lake on a sunny winter afternoon. This would also give him the opportunity to search many miles of shelf ice on the off chance of stumbling onto Tristan Laird.

"Trust me. I'm a doctor. If anything does happen to you, well, I'll do what I can. And if that fails, I'll give you absolution."

"Are you a...."

"No, but when I started college, I was a drama major. I'll give a convincing performance."

"You've got your drysuit?" asked Ray.

"Everything is in the car. Just point me in the direction of some place I can change."

"There's a bathroom and a guest room through there. Take your choice," said Ray. "I need to check the weather on NOAA and local radar. Then I'll get changed."

"Go ahead, I'll clear up the dishes and get my things," she said.

Thirty minutes later, dressed in drysuits and mukluks, they were off-loading the kayaks—long, slender boats designed for use in big waves and rough water—and carrying them to the snow-covered bank of a small stream. Then they donned thick neoprene spray skirts, stepping into tunnels and doing a little dance as they struggled to pull the skirts to their waists. Next they added bright yellow life vests, the pockets on each stuffed with gear.

"Looks like we'll have the lake to ourselves. No other kayakers."

"Not many people venture out in these conditions," said Ray.

"What are you going to do about a hat?" Jeffers asked.

"When the water is this temperature, I always wear this neoprene hood. You never know when you're going to get capsized," said Ray. He pulled his on, centering the opening, exposing little more than his eyes, nose, and mouth.

"You've persuaded me to do the same, I'll just have to live with helmet-head hair," she said. She pulled off a black stocking cap and retrieved a heavy neoprene hood from her gear bag. "Are you going to wear a tow rope or put it on your deck?" she asked.

"Better to wear it," answered Ray as he turned on and checked his VHF radio, returning it to the top, left-hand pocket of his life vest. Once they had all their gear attached to the decks of their boats—extra paddles, hydration packs, cell phones in watertight bags—they slid into their boats and secured their spray skirts to their cockpit coamings, creating a watertight unit. After pulling on thick neoprene mittens, they seal-launched into the water, sliding down icy banks. They carefully negotiated the twisting path the stream had cut through the shelf ice that extended more than fifty yards out past the beach. The forward edge rose more than ten feet above the water, built up by floating ice being piled up during violent winter storms. Finally they emerged onto the big lake, the enormous stretch of water, the curve of the planet visible on the vista where the dark water met the lighter sky.

"Wow, this is incredible. The view always knocks me on my ass," Hannah observed. "Where to, chief?"

"Where do you want to go?"

"You're the guide."

"Let's start toward that headland, Empire Hill." Ray motioned with his hand. "That's about 10 miles. We can turn back whenever you've had enough or it looks like the weather might be changing."

"What did NOAA say?"

"For the rest of the afternoon, winds from the southwest at five to ten, waves one foot or less. But there's a system coming in and things should start picking up before dark. As you can see, given the steep face of the shelf ice, there aren't many places to bail out along here if the weather deteriorates. We've got to be vigilant."

"Does your radio have the 'weather alert' feature?" Hannah asked.

"It's turned on," he answered. "That said, sometimes the weather is on you before an alert is issued."

They started north, moving quickly in the gentle swell. Ray was happy to note that Jeffers was a strong and skilled kayaker. He usually picked his paddling companions carefully, especially in conditions that might become challenging or dangerous.

"I'd like to do a couple of rolls. Will you spot for me?" asked Jeffers.

"Are you ready for an ice cream headache?" Ray responded.

"I haven't rolled in cold water for a while. I need to know that I can do it." She pulled some nose clips from her vest, checked the position of the release strap on her spray skirt, and looked over at Ray, who had positioned the bow of his kayak a few paddle strokes off the center of her boat.

"Ready?" she asked.

"Yes," he said, prepared to quickly move in and give her his bow to pull up on if she missed her roll.

Jeffers sat up straight, slowly took a couple of deep breaths, then made a forceful lean to the right, capsizing the boat. She almost righted the boat on her first attempt, falling back at the last moment. Ray watched as she set up a second time and successfully rolled. "What's the problem?" she asked, after coughing a couple of times.

"You brought your head up too fast the first time."

"Damn, I always do that when I'm out of practice. I'm going to try a couple more."

Jeffers performed a series of smooth, elegant rolls.

"Those looked good," said Ray. "It's a good thing to practice, especially in these conditions. It's easy to ride up on some submerged ice and get flipped."

They headed north again, picking up the pace to warm up after her submersion in the icy water. They stopped along the way to explore some of the bigger ice caves, Jeffers capturing interesting configurations with her camera, Ray carefully checking for signs that Tristan Laird might have been there. He saw none.

The hours quickly passed as they paddled and played along in the ornate ice sculptures. Suddenly, Ray's radio came to life. He stopped paddling and listened to the alert, which was repeated several times.

"I didn't get all of it," said Jeffers.

"They've just posted small craft advisories, looks like that front's coming in sooner than expected. We better get going," Ray cautioned.

They turned south again.

A thin overcast had moved in dulling the delicate afternoon light, and beyond it Ray could see a long band of heavy dark clouds. The wind had started to pick up, and the wave heights were increasing. What had been a leisurely paddle became a dash for their launch site before the conditions completely deteriorated. There was little banter; just two seasoned paddlers focused on getting safely back on land before dark.

The sun disappeared in the gray overcast as the wind and waves increased.

14

As they began to battle the wind and surf, they moved into deeper water, away from the reflecting waves coming off the ice shelf. Ray took a more direct heading on the curved bay toward their launch site. Slowly the miles slipped by and their destination grew larger.

Ray panned the shoreline, making adjustments to their course and constantly monitoring his companion, who seemed little bothered by the rough water. Every time his bow broke through a wave, Ray was showered by a freezing spray of water. Ice built up on the deck and clung to the lines, bungee cords, and his spray skirt. When he could clearly see their goal, little more than a mile away, he started to relax a bit, knowing that in about fifteen or twenty minutes they would be safely on land.

He was thinking about Tristan Laird, wondering where he was, and hoping he wasn't camping out in an ice cave. As his boat rose and fell in the increasing swell, he scanned the shoreline, his attention suddenly pulled to objects and motion on the water near the shelf ice. He turned his bow in that direction, trying to understand what he was seeing, his vision often obscured by the waves.

"We've got company," he shouted. "Let's take a closer look."

They started paddling toward the dark forms, kayaks. As they neared they both could tell something was wrong.

"Looks like trouble," Jeffers yelled.

As they approached the kayaks they could see four boats, three with occupants, one capsized. The paddlers were struggling to control their boats in the surf and the swirl of reflecting waves rebounding off the shelf ice. As they drew closer, Ray could see a figure bobbing in a life vest near the capsized kayak. The other members of the group, fighting to remain upright, could offer little assistance to the swimmer.

Ray and Jeffers sprinted toward the form in the water.

As they drew closer, Ray began to assess the situation. A group of kids, teenagers, in small recreational kayaks. They appeared to be wearing ski parkas under their life vests. He imagined that they were probably wearing jeans, nothing to protect them from the effects of the frigid water.

Ray took control of the scene, yelling at the three boaters to move to deeper water, away from the swimmer, a girl who was flailing around in the surf, struggling to keep her head above the surface. Ray went to retrieve the kayak, while Jeffers paddled to the swimmer.

He tried to right the craft. Without floatation or bulkheads, the water-filled boat barely broke the surface. Ray tried to pull the kayak onto his foredeck, but quickly realized that he didn't have the strength to fight the hundreds of pounds of water that flooded its interior. He pushed it off his deck.

Ray paddled next to Jeffers, who was holding onto one of the straps of the swimmer's life vest at the other side of her boat. He ramped his boat against hers.

"What's her condition?"

"Deteriorating fast, barely responsive. It's rush, rush."

"We'll get her on your deck, and I'll try to tow you the rest of the way. Think you can hold her?"

"Yes. She's small."

Ray reached over Jeffer's deck, using her kayak to stabilize his. He pushed his neoprene mitten through a strap on the girl's vest and pulled her small frame across the decks of both boats and then positioned her on Hannah's boat, her chest flat on the bow deck, feet dangling, one on each side, facing Hannah.

"Sure you can hold her?"

"Yes."

While they were still ramped, Ray pulled out his radio, and keyed the transmit button, repeating "Mayday" three times. There was an instant response. He gave their location and nature of the emergency, and waited briefly for a comeback.

Then he pushed his boat forward, clipping his towrope to the loop on the front of Jeffers' boat and paddling away from the shelf ice, the line spooling out of his tow bag, then growing taut, several feet of thick shock cord at the end of the line dampening the pull of the rope. He yelled at the other three kayakers to follow them, hoping that they could make it in safely without anyone else capsizing.

He had about a mile to cover, ten or twelve minutes in flat water, but in these waves and wind and towing a bow-heavy boat, he struggled to move forward. Ray could feel the adrenalin kicking in as he struggled through the deepening troughs, hoping that Jeffers would not be capsized. Ray glanced occasionally back at her and the other paddlers.

As he neared the opening to the river, he could see figures standing on the shelf ice. He paddled beyond the opening and then headed straight in, the trailing boat following him into the river. By the time he was near the shore, firefighters, dressed in cold-water rescue suits, scrambled into the water. They pulled Jeffers' boat up the bank, and then quickly moved the victim to a stretcher. Ray caught a glimpse of Jeffers following the stretcher toward the waiting ambulance.

Then he released his spray skirt and pulled himself out of the cockpit, near exhaustion and struggling to get to his feet. Two firefighters helped him up the embankment and retrieved his kayak for him. He sat on the bank and watched as they got the other three boaters, two boys and a girl onto the shore. Ray wanted to scream at the kids, but he only sat, struggling to catch his breath.

An hour later Ray caught up with Jeffers. She was standing and working at a keyboard in the large open area of the trauma center that was surrounded by treatment rooms, her yellow and blue drysuit looking out of place against the sea of pale green scrubs.

"You okay?" she asked.

"Tired," he responded.

"I'm almost done here," she said, looking up and smiling.

"How's the patient?" he asked.

"She's responding well, but it was a close one." After a few key-strokes, she looked up again. "Okay, I'm logged off, and we're out of here."

As they walked toward the car, Jeffers asked, "How did you know where to find the keys?"

"I saw you put them in a dry bag that you stashed in your day hatch before we launched."

"And you drove here on your own. If you'd had a stroke along the way you could have destroyed both my car and my kayak."

Ray handed her the keys. "Yeah, it's your lucky day." He collapsed into the passenger seat, happy to be chauffeured. After a few miles he asked, "How close was it?"

"Close, another ten or fifteen minutes in the water, and she'd have been gone," she said, watching the oncoming traffic as she waited to make a left turn. "By tomorrow this will just be a bad dream. Although I bet she's probably given up winter kayaking for life."

Ray was too tired to respond.

"What if we'd had four swimmers?" Jeffers asked. "What if the four swimmers had capsized us in their desperation?"

"We were lucky," he said.

There was little conversation for the rest of trip, and Hannah Jeffers stayed only long enough to change out of her drysuit. She explained that she needed to get back to her apartment to shower and get some sleep before she went back on call at midnight.

15

Ray was startled when he looked at the clock on the stove as he began to make coffee. He was always up early, even on the weekend, an internal clock pulling him to consciousness every morning between five and six o'clock. But on this Sunday morning he had slept in and not by intention. And even with all the extra sleep, he was still feeling weary, his body sore from the events of the last few days.

As he sat at the table eating oatmeal and sipping coffee, he studied two maps, one pinpointing the location of Tristan Laird's trailer, the other showing the possible location of a tree house that Molly Birchard had identified as one of Tristan's hideaways. Her directions to the second location were less exact. The place marked on the map was Molly's best guess of where it might be, a remote piece of private land near the south end of the Sleeping Bear Dunes National Lakeshore.

Ray decided that he would start with the trailer first, since the tree house would probably be impossible to find given Molly's rather fuzzy description of its location. He opened his laptop to check the weather and temperature so he would know how to dress for his outing. Then he looked at his email. Finally there was a note from Sarah sent from her Blackberry apologizing for being incommunicado. She explained that she was at O'Hare waiting for an early morning flight. She asked if he was available for dinner this evening, noting that she would bring dessert.

He quickly keyed a response, saying he'd love to make dinner for her, suggesting five o'clock.

As soon as he hit the send button, his thoughts turned to the menu and things that were on hand or had to be purchased at the market on his way back from the trek in search of Tristan Laird. He pulled a lamb rib roast from the freezer and put it in the sink to defrost. Then he looked through the contents of the refrigerator. The possible makings for a salad were mostly dead, and there were no fresh vegetables. When he checked a bag of petite potatoes, he found that they had started to sprout. It immediately became clear that other than the lamb, the menu would depend on what he found at the local market.

The road into Tristan's was exactly as marked. Ray had brought both skis and snowshoes. Given the heavy covering of snow and the deep drifts, including the several inches of fresh powder that fell the previous afternoon and evening, he decided that the snowshoes would be the most efficient way to get to his destination. As he started up the road, there were no hints of tire ruts or snowmobile tracks, not even animal tracks, just the even blanket of snow, several months of accumulation, layers on top of another, collapsing with age and weight.

As he worked his way along the narrow trail, the brilliant sunshine that had put him in an ebullient mood started to disappear. Soon the sky went gray and snow began to fall, a gentle dusting.

Ray guessed that this road was barely passable during the best of times. Trees and bushes had made a steady incursion in the seldom-used trail, and there were places in a low, swampy area where it had all but disappeared.

Ray found the dwelling at the terminus of the track, a sagging house trailer with a flimsy rust-covered set of stairs leaning into the structure just below an entry door. Cloaked in snow, firewood was stacked on each side of the stairs. The front and back walls of the trailer were raked in from the roof to the floor, a failed attempt at modern design dating from the '50s.

An old Toyota pickup truck, the body propped high over the wheels, stood some distance from the trailer. It was covered by a heavy mantle of snow, suggesting it hadn't been moved for months. Ray wondered if it was in running condition.

The entrance door was secured by a large, brass padlock that dangled from a badly corroded hasp. Ray could see that someone had made an effort to reinforce the right side of the doorframe near the area. A crudely shaped piece of wood, probably oak, had been secured by lag screws over the side of the hasp to protect it from being pried away from its mounting screws. He suspected the interior had been similarly reinforced.

The vandalizing of remote seasonal homes and hunting cabins was a common occurrence, especially during the winter months when even the most secluded locations were easily accessible by snowmobile. The more remote the location, the more time the vandals had to kick down doors or tear through walls or windows. Usually by the time the owners discovered the damage, weeks or months had passed and any evidence that might lead the police to the culprits was long gone. Ray suspected that most of this was done by young men, either locals or from downstate, who ranged through the area in the dead of winter, often at night, enjoying an alcohol and testosterone-fired wildness that would put them behind bars under normal circumstances.

Ray circled the trailer in a clockwise direction. There was no skirt at the base and he could see that occasional stacks of concrete blocks provided the foundation for the trailer. There was no evidence that anyone had been near the structure. He moved close to the structure, trying to see into the interior. Faded, tattered curtains almost completely obstructed his view. Two rust- covered propane tanks stood at the front of the trailer, unconnected to the couplers and oxidized copper tubing. He could see the washed out remains of the manufacturer's logo, a crescent shape and the words *New Moon*. He noted the irony.

Ray completed his circuit and moved away from the building, stopping to look back at the scene for a long moment. The reclusive Tristan Laird clearly had not been at this location for a long time.

As he worked his way back toward the highway, he grew aware of how quickly he was becoming fatigued. Lifting the snowshoes at each step became increasingly arduous. He was greatly relieved to see his vehicle slowly taking form in the distance. He glanced at his watch. The search for Tristan Laird was over for the day.

16

~~~~~~~~

Walking across the parking lot at the market, Ray, sore and stiff, moved with difficulty. Once inside the store, he grabbed a cart and headed toward the produce section to look for salad ingredients. During the growing season, locally produced greens and fruits fresh from nearby farms were a specialty of this family-owned store, but in the dead of winter, most of the produce on display looked travel weary, even with the constant misting from overhead sprayers.

Ray looked through the sealed boxes of organic lettuce, noting the edges were less than crisp. He finally settled on a round container of bib, the blurb on the top purporting that the product within had survived the long trip from California. Next he examined the tomatoes, which were either green or starting to wither with age. The avocadoes were rock hard to the touch. Finally he found some pears, products of a South American summer. He thought the lettuce, pears, some walnuts, and the last bit of his stash of Stilton, combined with a dash of olive oil and lime balsamic vinegar would make an acceptable salad. Then he grabbed a package of fresh thyme and a bag of petite potatoes, checking first to see that the spuds hadn't started to sprout like the ones in his refrigerator. He glanced at the rows of wine bottles and then his watch, deciding quickly to go with whatever he had at home. Finally he selected a baguette, a day old and damaged by time, but somewhat repairable with a few minutes in a hot oven.

Walking back toward his car, Ray felt like he was starting to move with greater ease. And once he was home, as he busied himself with the preparation of the meal, he forgot about his sore muscles.

By the time Sarah arrived, he'd made the salad and the potatoes were boiled and ready to go into the oven with the lamb. After a long hug, Ray said, "Glad you're here. I've missed you."

"I've missed you, too. And there's a special gift from Chicago for you," she pointed at a square cardboard bakery box. "That wasn't easy to get through security."

"You do look a bit like the Unabomber," said Ray, cutting through the tape and carefully opening the box. He peered at the tart, a fine lattice of pastry dividing individual raspberries, each one perfectly formed and ripe, nature's beauty enhanced by a glistening glaze.

"I don't think I can eat this," said Ray in a joking tone.

"Why not?"

"It's too beautiful. I think I'll frame it."

"I know you love raspberries, too bad they didn't have thimbleberries. I got the tart at a highly recommended French bakery near my apartment building. Sorry about bringing day-old baked goods, but you do what you can do."

"Your apartment, so much has happened. Tell me about it."

"What do you want to know?"

"Tell me about the job, the apartment, what your life is going to be like." As the words slipped from his lips, Ray was starting to think about what his life would be like without Sarah living close by, a topic he had been avoiding thinking about since she first mentioned it a few days before. Over the last several months, Sarah had been with him through a difficult period of loss and physical injury, and Ray had started to assume that she would continue to become an increasingly important part of his life. But with this sudden change of jobs, everything was now in flux.

"So tell me about the job," he said again, trying to make conversation.

"Don't I get a glass of wine first?"

"I thought we'd start with one of Mawby's sparkling wines," said Ray, carefully removing the wire and foil, then covering the cork with a dish towel and carefully turning it until a controlled pop ended the process.

He filled two hollow-stemmed glasses, passed Sarah one, carefully grasped the second one and offered a toast, "Here's to your new job."

"Thank you," she said, sipping the wine and setting the glass on the counter. "Where did you get these glasses? They are so delicate, and I love the art nouveau look."

"They were a housewarming gift from Nora."

"I should have known Nora was the source, they're twice as big as any other champagne glasses."

Ray continued, "She remembered how much I admired them over the years, and brought six glasses and a very good bottle of Champagne. She said she got the glasses 50 some years ago as a wedding present, from a grandmother or aunt. Nora said at her age she'd never be entertaining again at a level where she'd need a dozen champagne glasses, and I should enjoy them."

Sarah picked up the bottle, looking at the scarlet label and gold lettering, "So clever, you men," she commented.

There was a lull in the conversation. Ray noted an unnatural tension between them as he prepared the salad. "Tell me about the job," he asked a third time, needing to fill the silence.

"The job is as described. It's a management job. It will be very different."

"How so?" Ray asked after he finished spinning the lettuce.

"As you know, at Leiston I do a bit of everything. That won't be the case in the Chicago job. There I'm to coordinate the work of the support staff management team. Specialists are in place in the various support areas. My charge is to make everything in the office run smoothly so the lawyers get what they need. It's all about improving their efficiency, billable hours, and opportunity to make money."

"So what were you doing the last few days?"

"Friday I was on the plane at seven, got there at seven, and was in the office by eight central time. I was shown around and introduced to people, and I was wined and dined at lunch and dinner. I can't imagine what the bill was at Charlie Trotters.

Yesterday morning I was offered a contract, and there was a little back and forth on the terms. The initial offer was incredibly generous,

and the few extras I asked for were met. It's such an adjustment coming from education," she observed. "The secretaries at the firm make a
lot more than the senior teachers at Leiston."

Sarah refilled her glass and topped up Ray's. "Then the firm's concierge started to arrange things for me."

"Concierge?"

"That's not exactly her title, but that's what she is, a smart young
woman just out of Princeton; she's taking a year or two off before she
starts law school. She makes things happen for the partners so they can
focus on law and not be bothered with travel plans, or concert tickets
or..."

"So what did she do for you?"

"Phoebe, that's her name, has studied what makes relocation difficult for people, and she helps with all those things. I now have sugges-
tions for a new dentist, gynecologist, and internist. And I know where
to get my hair and nails done. They're all located close to the office and
my apartment, which is furnished unless I want to move in my own
things. I'm also clear on the unwritten dress code and what stores I
should shop at. And she filled me in on lots of other things I should
know to avoid possible problems."

"Like what?"

"You know, Ray, sometimes I don't really think that we have conversations. I feel like I'm being interrogated."

He was silent for a long moment, thinking about what Sarah had just
said and how she had said it. "I'm just interested in your life," he said,
defensively. In the months he had known Sarah, he had never heard
her use that tone of voice before.

"Phoebe was telling me things I needed to know, environmental
factors, like who to avoid—the office neurotics, lechers, and crazies.
And then we spent some time at the apartment. Phoebe is coordinating
the move."

Ray made thin slices from the baguette he had just pulled from the
oven and arranged them on a plate around a ramekin with a smoked
salmon and cream cheese spread he'd found in the back of the refrigerator. Sarah took some more champagne, pausing to see how much
the bottle contained.

"I remember you telling me about the apartment, but I don't remember the details. And I apologize if you've told me before. Things are sort of hazy. I was on some medication."

"It's two blocks from the office. It's great, fourteenth floor, unrestricted view of the lake."

"And why are they...?"

"They want me close to the office. Depending on what's going on, like some of the lawyers being in trial, some members of the support staff often work nights and weekends. It's my job to coordinate that, even fill in if needed."

Ray had several questions. Would she be able to come north for weekends, could he visit her in Chicago? He held back. "Are you ready for dinner?" he asked. "It will be about twenty minutes after I put the lamb in the oven."

"Go ahead. Food would be good. I think the champagne is getting to me," she answered, excusing herself and heading off to the guest bathroom.

Ray slid the two racks of lamb ribs that had been marinating in olive oil and fresh rosemary into the oven and set the timer. He retrieved a meat thermometer from a drawer and placed it on the counter near the oven. Then he took a sip of his champagne and reflected on his conversation with Sarah. Thus far there had been no mention of how he might fit into her new life.

Ray watched Sarah return to the room holding something in her right hand. He could tell by her expression and body language, something was very wrong. She lifted her hand so Ray could see a delicate material in a leopard skin pattern. "To whom do these belong?" she asked.

"What do you have?" he asked innocently.

"They seem to be long johns, silk, women's." She held them out and looked at the label. "In a petite."

"Where did you find them?"

"Hanging in the bath over the shower bar."

"I have no idea," Ray said. He could see his response only further enflamed the situation. And then he put things together. "Oh, those."

"Oh, those," she responded in a mocking tone.

"I went kayaking with a doctor from the hospital yesterday. She changed out of her drysuit before she left and must have tossed them there and forgotten them."

"So here is a man who's been hospitalized for passing out, perhaps related to a horrific event, and two days later he's off kayaking with a leopard-skin clad woman. Ray Elkins, you have remarkable recuperative powers."

"Let me explain…."

"And I'm really tired. I need to go home."

"How about the dinner I've prepared. The lamb is almost done."

"I've got to go."

"You should have some food. You've had a lot of champagne."

"I'm okay," she said, gathering up her things.

Ray watched the door close behind her. The timer on the oven sounded.

17

Ray was adding information to his whiteboard diagram when Sue entered his office a little after eight on Monday morning.

"I came by your place to pick you up, but I could tell by the tracks in the snow you had already left. So much for doctor's orders."

"How was Grand Rapids?" Ray asked.

"I trust you kicked back Saturday afternoon and yesterday and got some rest."

"Absolutely. How was Grand Rapids?" he asked a second time.

"Brenda Manton, following her relatives instructions, will be pulled off a respirator sometime today."

"Tell me about her family."

"I met both brothers and their wives and her mother. Good people, smart, very solid. Brenda was probably the outlier, the artsy one in a family of professionals. That said, from my conversations with them I sensed that they respected what she did. They all seem to be high-performing people, and the more I learn about her, she seems to fit that mold also."

"Did you learn anything from them that might help us find her assailant?"

"No, not really. I talked to them at length, and I didn't sense that anyone was holding anything back. For them this violence was unfathomable. They couldn't imagine how this happened."

"Did you learn anything more about Brenda?"

"I'm not sure how much they know about her. I didn't sense that they were estranged, but neither were they close. They are all busy people pursuing their own lives. Her mother told me that Brenda came down for a couple of days at Christmas. She also said that she would see Brenda often during the summer. They have a family cottage on Glen Lake where her mother spends most weekends during the summer. If there are any dark secrets in Brenda's life, her siblings and mother are probably not aware of them."

"Did you find a home for Simone?"

"I took her along—she loves car rides. I told them that she was in the car and that I had been looking after her, and she was a wonderful dog. They didn't show any interest in taking Simone." Sue paused for a moment. "I don't know if I have time for a dog, but we're starting to bond."

"So what are the plans now? A funeral, memorial service?"

"They are talking about a memorial service next summer at their cottage. And this is where it gets quite interesting. Our Molly was there, and so was Elise Lovell who helped Brenda on the church project. I think that they came together. Molly, who had mostly been in the background trying to be supportive and helpful, got rather animated over this issue. She wants them to have a service for Brenda at that new big-box church down at the end of the county, the church that replaced Reverend Tim's *Freewill Bikers Bible Church* or whatever it was called."

"As I remember it," said Ray, "the complete name was the *Freewill Bible Synod of God, the Only True Followers of Jesus* or something close to that. The *Jesus loves Bikers* was just tacked onto the original sign."

"Yes, that's the place. What do you know about the new building or church?"

"Not much," Ray answered. "I haven't talked to Reverend Tim in awhile. I heard that someone with deep pockets bought his church and was building a new church, and that somehow Reverend Tim is still involved. So what does Molly want the family to do? I don't understand."

"This is the interesting part," said Sue. "Seems Brenda's last major commission was working on the interior of the new church. Molly was trying to convince Brenda's family that having a memorial service at the new church would be just wonderful because the walls are covered with Brenda's most recent and best work. She went on and on about the great minister there."

Ray looked incredulous.

"Molly's not really your type," Sue said to Ray.

"Where did that come from?" asked Ray.

"I don't know. I saw a lot more of her in Grand Rapids than ever before. She's pretty ditzy. I'm remembering how you responded to her when she wouldn't get to the point." She paused. "Let me explain, and first I have to say that you are enormously accepting and non-judgmental. It's just that I've observed that some personality types bug you. And watching Molly with Brenda's mother and brothers, well she started to bug me too. She was just too aggressive. And her thinking is scattered and illogical.

"On the drive back I was thinking about our talks with her and your feeling that she was holding a lot back, that she wasn't really being honest with us. I'm with you on that, especially now. And the way she was pushing for this memorial service at the Freewill Whatever was totally inappropriate. She was obnoxious."

"So how did it end up?" asked Ray.

"I left before any decision had been made."

"Was Elise Lovell a participant in this discussion?"

"Not really. She didn't say much and seemed rather embarrassed by Molly's behavior," Sue answered.

"We need to talk to Elise," said Ray. "And we need to find out about Brenda's work at this church. Maybe there's some connection there." Ray pointed at the whiteboard, and then pulled a marker off the tray below the board.

"We know so little about Brenda or her links to the community. And we're going forward on the assumption that she knew her killer. But, as you know, we always have to keep in mind that this could have been a random event. Who knew a single woman was living alone in the middle of a forest? Look at the possibilities. The UPS and FedEx guys, the propane delivery driver, a snowmobiler that she chased off her property, a construction worker from..."

"And then there's the arson bit," Sue suggested.

"Do you have a report yet?"

"I've got an email from Mike Ogden confirming what we already know. A large quantity of gasoline was poured around the interior of her house and ignited. Mike thinks about four or five gallons."

"How about the snowplow?"

"Same there, the accelerant was also gasoline. And he also noted something I missed," said Sue.

"What was that?"

"The cap was pulled off the fuel tank. Mike speculated that the perp poured gasoline into the tank to make sure the diesel got ignited too, like they wanted to make sure the fire completely destroyed the truck. He found the fuel cap in the snow and took it back to the lab to check for prints."

"Anything?"

"No." Sue looked at the board. "What's our plan?"

"I need to do some paperwork to keep this department running. That should take about an hour. Jan has all the work organized, I just need to read and sign. Then I'd like to find out more about this church and Brenda's work there. So let's start with Reverend Tim and get him to show us around and introduce us to the new preacher. If there's still some light left, we take a hike in the woods and look for Tristan Laird."

"Wouldn't it be easier and faster to take a couple of snowmobiles? We could cover a lot of ground quickly. I could have Brett meet us with the sleds."

"If this guy is as skittish as Molly says, he'll hear us coming. Let's take skis and snowshoes and make a decision on what to use when we get there."

"You really hate snowmobiles," opined Sue.

Ray let her comment slide. "And then let's try to talk to Molly again this evening. She's on tonight?"

"I'll check. She would normally start at eleven. I'll see if she will come in at ten."

"That should be enough time. For tomorrow, let's interview Elise Lovell. And would you organize someone to do a canvassing of anyone who might have had contact with Manton. It's pretty sparse out there, but maybe she knew some of her neighbors. And who were the delivery and service people she might have had contact with?"

"I'll have Brett do that. It'll be a good learning experience for him."

"Okay, we've got a plan of sorts. Let's try to get out of here by ten."

After Sue left, Ray returned to his paperwork. His efforts were quickly interrupted by his cell phone ringing. Sarah's face came on the screen.

"Ray, are you okay?"

"Yes."

"I'm so sorry about last night. I embarrassed myself. I was sort of a crazy lady. I don't deal well with change, and I'm struggling with our relationship, what's going to happen with the move. And I'd say let's get together tonight, but I've got to take the new headmaster and his assistants to dinner in town. One of the school's major benefactors is flying in, and I've got to be there."

"Let's play it by ear," offered Ray.

"Okay. I'll only be here a few days, and then I'm going to Chicago. I'll try to figure something out. Ray, I do care about you. I'll call you later."

"Good," he responded. The beeping sound indicated that Sarah had rung off.

18

"Do you want to drive up to that church or do you want to try Reverend Tim's house?" asked Sue.

"Let's try the house first," Ray answered.

Sue parked in front of an aging mobile home. "Wasn't that car engine hanging from that tree the last time we were here?"

"Hard to say," Ray responded. "It might have been a different engine. And maybe it isn't really an old V-8 hanging from a tree."

"What is it then?"

"Yard art, a post-modern deconstruction emblematic of the end of the industrial age."

The door of the trailer opened as they approached the porch.

"Sheriff, what brings you?"

"Reverend Tim, I haven't seen you for a long time. Lots of changes around here. Thought we could have a little talk."

"Well, come on in, you too, ma'am. I'll get some coffee going. Place is a bit of a mess. Wife's off looking after her father. I was down there most of last week. He broke his hip and lots of other stuff seems to be going wrong now."

They followed Tim into the trailer—the interior as dilapidated as the exterior. The furniture was worn and sagging. A woodstove stood in a small, tacked-on addition off the kitchen/living room. The interior smelled of smoke and stale food.

Reverend Tim seated them at the kitchen table and started talking at them while getting a percolator started on the gas stove. "Well, Sheriff, good that you came looking for me when you did. Another week or two this building and the old church will be gone."

"How's that?" asked Ray.

"Reverend Rod wants this and the old church building gone. He says things will look better. He's buying us a new doublewide. I'm going to put it on some land I own up the road a mile. Sure will miss this place. We've been here since we got married, raised kids here. It's been good."

He plunked three mugs on the table, pushing one in Ray's direction and one toward Sue.

"So give me some background, Tim. You had a church and a congregation here. And now there's that huge building up on the hill and another minister. Fill us in on what's happened."

Tim pulled the coffee pot off the stove and filled the mugs. He tossed two frayed hot pads on the worn Formica table and settled in his chair.

"It's really the strangest damn thing. God has his own way of doing things, but I don't quite understand what this is all about. I guess I need to learn patience."

"So what are you telling me, Tim?"

"Well, Reverend Rod shows up one day. I didn't know he was a preacher. He drives up in a BMW, not a bike, a car. If he'd been on one of those kinds of bikes I wouldn't even have bothered to listen to him. He tells me he's looking to buy a church and a congregation. At first I thought he was some yuppie summer person just giving me a line of bull for the fun of it. You know, he could go back and tell his friends over drinks about how he put one over on some old-time preacher. I was getting pretty rude, I wanted him to go away, but he just kept talking. And it all sounded like bull."

"So what happened?"

"I told him I wasn't interested, and he went away. But after he left I started thinking. You know my church is in a lot of trouble. I got left all this land when my dad died. He had inherited from his dad, my grand-dad, who bought it at a tax sale during the depression when it wasn't worth nothing. The lumber had been cut thirty, forty years before and then burned over. Back then in the thirties it was scrub oak, second growth.

"And after my dad died I hung on to most of the property. It was all listed as forest land, so the taxes weren't much. But the population is growing, and little by little the land has been growing in value. A number of years ago I started borrowing on it. The first time was to help get my wife an operation. I found out that it was pretty easy to do, borrowing money. And the bank manager, Charlie Cook, would always make a joke about cooking me up a great deal when I needed some cash. So none of this was a problem when things was good. I was doing lots of motorcycle and car repair and selling off some hardwoods from time to time. And then everything just sort of went bad, the economy and such. When I wasn't able to keep up on my payments, I went to see Charlie. Well, he'd been fired. And the woman that replaced him is something else. So it looked like I was going to get foreclosed.

"So this guy with the BMW comes back a few days later and starts talking to me again. He's got this idea about a new kind of church, but it would be good if he started with a church that was already successful. He gets me to take him around my property. We go up to the top of that hill over there. There's already a big clearing there where we clear-cut some hardwoods a few years back. And he says, 'This is it. This is where my church is meant to be.' Like he got some message from heaven or something. So I say maybe so, but I tell him the bank's got a lien on it.

"Well, Rod asks me how much and a couple of days later he picks me up, and we go to the bank. Rod writes a check, and I'm off the hook."

"Did you sell him the property?"

"Yes, I sold him this piece of property. Most of the money went to pay off the mortgage, but I did get something. We agreed that I could live here until the new building was finished."

"And you're working with this minister, this Rod...?" Sue asked.

"Yes, ma'am. I'm working there, but it ain't quite what I expected."

"How so?" asked Sue.

"When Rod talked about it at first, it was like we was going to be sort of equals, but the truth is that I'm in the sidecar. It's his church, his operation, his money. I still minister to my flock, people I've known most of my life. I do home and hospital visits and some weddings and funerals. I don't get to preach in the new church. I got sort of a two-year contract, but..."

"But what?"

Reverend Tim was slow to respond. "Well, this isn't my kind of religion. And I don't think he is what he told me. He's got lots of new ideas that don't fit with the good old religion that's always worked for me and my flock."

"I'm not quite following you, Reverend Tim," said Ray. "What is Rod ... does he have a last name?"

"His last name is Gunne. It sounds like gun, but it's got an extra 'ne' at the end. And the thing that bothers me, well, there's lots of things that bother me. First, what happens at the services is all 'bout what goes into his TV cameras. It's all about his Webcasts and things looking good."

"Reverend Tim, I'm not quite sure what you're talking about."

"It's like this, Sheriff, I used to deliver old religion, teaching the gospel, doing baptisms in the creek back there," he motioned with his hand. "This what he's doing ain't nothing like that. He's always talking about brand. What the hell's brand? And image. And 'a new paradigm for bringing the Word.' And Twitter, and Facebook, and all that stuff.

"Let me tell you, one of the first things he did was recruit some of my flock to be his main TV people. He picked them from the group, got them haircuts and clothes and sat them all together. I couldn't believe it when I saw the recording of that service. You see Rod giving his service and you see this group of people, not anyone else in the church, camera never shows anyone else. And they're so fixed up they don't even look like themselves, they almost look like summer people. And he keeps using that over and over in his weekly programs, Webcasts as he calls them. The same pictures of the same people when they was all dolled up. I tried to talk to him about it being phony and all, but he just says that's how video production works. And that's just the beginning."

"The other things?" pressed Ray.

"The big thing is that he doesn't really care about these people. He only thinks about his audience on the Internet. I mean, he calls the place The Church for the Next Millennium. He doesn't allow people to talk in tongues, says that's the wrong image and doesn't look good.

Sheriff, this ain't my kind of religion. Sorry if I've told you more than you wanted to know. I guess I've needed to get this off my chest. You're probably here for some other reason."

"In the new building I understand there's a lot of work by an area artist, wall hangings made of wool."

"Yeah, they're all over. It's sorta like really good shag carpeting, nice colors and design and all, but it don't make any sense."

"How so?"

"Well, there's not pictures from the Bible or anything like you should find in a church. Rod says it's representational. Like it shows God's glory in its colors and textures. And at the front, behind the altar, does he have a cross? No. Just this huge, round piece of painted aluminum made by some woman from around Detroit. Rod says it celebrates all that God has created, the unity of the planet, the unity of all living things. To me, it looks like a big hubcap, 60s Pontiac."

"Did you meet the artist, the woman who made the wall hangings?"

"Oh, yeah. Brenda, that's the woman, was around a lot. She had a crew, employed some of the ladies from the church, too. She'd have a design, and they'd do the sewing or whatever you call it. And then she directed how the rugs or whatever were put up."

"Did you hear that Brenda was injured in a home invasion?"

"No, Sheriff. Like I said, I've been in Kentucky for a week with my wife. Came back late last night. Was she hurt bad?"

"Real bad, she's not going to make it," said Ray. "We're running down leads, looking for any information that might help us find the assailant."

"That's just awful. Nice woman," said Reverend Tim. He raised his arms over his head, Moses like, and looked toward the heavens, and said, "Sometimes it's hard to understand the workings of the Lord."

"Can you think of anyone who would want to hurt her?"

"No, Sheriff. I didn't understand her art, but she's a nice person, real nice."

"Reverend Tim, we'd like to meet Rod Gunne. Would you take us up there and introduce us?"

"I'd be happy to. Let me get my coat, toss another log in the stove."

19

Sue drove up the wide, carefully plowed drive that opened into a huge parking lot that circled a large square building more than two stories high. She parked by a cluster of vehicles near the front entrance. As they emerged from her Jeep, Reverend Tim pulled his worn Dodge pickup near them.

"Lots of cars," said Ray. "Something going on?"

"No, that's just Rod's staff. He needs lots of folks to do all the Internet stuff and handle the money."

They entered the church through a large revolving door. "That door, energy savings," offered Tim. "Rod believes in all that junk science."

As they came through the second set of doors, Ray and Sue were struck by the brilliant interior. The central atrium extended from one side of the building to the other. On the wall on the right, between several sets of double doors that opened to the main auditorium, were large pieces of fabric art, each carefully lit by a series of strategically placed spotlights. They took their time moving from one panel to the next, absorbing the power and dimension of each piece.

"They're supposed to represent the dunes, the shoreline, the lake, and the islands," offered Tim in a docent-like manner.

On the opposite wall, above the line of the doors, was a continuous panel of LCD screens showing views of some of the planet's most spectacular natural settings. The scenes were moving and photographed from above, suggesting that they had been filmed from an aircraft.

"Come on into the sanctuary," Tim directed. They followed him.

"As you can see, there's no real pulpit. There is that lectern off to the side. But most of the time Rod just stands out there. If you're at the back of the church, you can see him on those screens." Tim pointed to a series of large screens on the side walls. "Rod says if you want to get people out of sports bars and into church, you got to make church better than the sports bars."

"How do you feel about that?" asked Ray.

"Tell you the truth," Reverend Tim said in a quiet voice, "I don't think they're the same thing. We're trying to get men's souls, not just their attention."

"Where do we find Mr. Gunne?" Ray asked, after peering at his watch.

"Follow me, I'll give you the Cook's tour on the way."

They crossed the atrium again and entered an office complex. They paused briefly at each door as Tim identified the different work areas: media production, marketing, computing, donor services, the nursery and Sunday school area, and finally the administrative offices.

They entered an office suite that looked like a high-end law office: thick carpeting, walnut paneling, and elegant furniture. "Shirley," said Tim, addressing a petite brunette in a carefully tailored suit, "is Reverend Rod available?"

The woman held Ray and Sue in her gaze for a long moment, and then looked back at Tim and replied. "I'll see," she answered, her tone flat, without affect. Leaving her desk, she disappeared down a hallway. A minute later she reappeared, "Follow me, please."

They were ushered into a tastefully decorated office. "Sheriff Elkins and Miss..." Tim looked at Ray for help.

"Detective Sergeant Sue Lawrence," Ray provided Sue's title.

"Rodney Gunne," said the man as he stood. He buttoned his suit coat and came around the side of a long modern desk. He shook hands with Ray, briefly making eye contact, and then carefully scrutinized Sue, taking her hand and holding it briefly.

"The Sheriff's here to talk about that woman who did all that artwork," Reverend Tim explained.

"I've just learned about that situation," said Gunne. "Most tragic. She's already in our prayers." He looked at Reverend Tim, "Thank you

for escorting the sheriff and Ms. Lawrence in. I'll see you later today."
His eyes moved to his secretary, "Shirley, hold my calls and catch the
door as you leave, please."

At Gunne's direction they settled into two large leather chairs that
faced his desk, and he returned to his chair.

"How can I be of assistance, Sheriff?"

"What do you know about Brenda Manton's condition?" asked Ray.

"I've just learned about this. I had a call from Elise Lovell. She was
Ms. Manton's assistant during the creation and installation of that
wonderful fabric art. Apparently Elise was with the family this weekend. I understand that Brenda will be taken off the machines and allowed to die sometime today." Gunne brought his hands together in
front of his chest in a prayer-like manner. "This is incredibly difficult
to comprehend. Brenda was such a gifted artist and such a wonderful
person. Some things are beyond human comprehension." After a long
pause, he asked, "How can I be of assistance, Sheriff?"

"We're in the early stages of the investigation, and we're talking to
anyone who has recently had contact with Brenda Manton. We're looking for anything that might help us identify who was responsible for
this crime."

"I don't know if I can be of much help. She was one of many contractors on this project," he opened his arms as though giving the
benediction.

"Why don't you just talk about her for awhile," urged Sue. "Give
us some background. Perhaps something will come to you that might
prove to be helpful. How did you meet Manton?"

"When I was called to this project, I wanted to break all of the para-
digms and construct a very different place of worship. I didn't want
any of the old iconography, and I didn't want to use materials that you
usually find in a religious building. As the name implies, this church
represents a new kind of relationship with God. We offer a new and
positive message. I wanted the building to reflect this ministry."

"How did you meet Brenda?"

"I was just getting to that, Sheriff. I saw a few small pieces of her
work at a gallery in Birmingham." As he spoke, he looked directly at
Ray, only occasionally making eye contact with Sue. "I had gone down
state to meet with my decorator to get ideas. I loved Manton's work and

wondered if she could scale it up to my vision of our interior wall coverings. I was surprised to find out that she lived locally.

"She came to visit when the building was little more than a steel exoskeleton. She's a wiz at computers and computer art. She quickly produced renderings of what her art would look like and how she would place it and light it. I was knocked over the first time I saw them on that big laptop she was always carrying. We were on the same page right from the beginning. She was totally empathic to what I was trying to attain. So for a period of time we were almost in daily contact, but since her work was completed I've only seen her occasionally. Brenda sometimes brought prospective clients here. This is the single biggest installation of her art."

"Have you ever been to her house?" asked Sue.

"Early on, yes, only a few times. She would design the panels, and she would show me what she was proposing on a huge screen she had."

"Have you been there recently?" Ray asked.

"No, not in months. There was no need. Her work was completed."

"So you didn't form a friendship beyond her work here?"

"No, Ms. Lawrence. I like to think that we, Brenda and I, were friends, but our relationship was professional. That said, she was a person I greatly admired. And what has happened is incomprehensible."

"Did she ever share any fears or anxieties?"

"Nothing like that."

"Might she have formed a relationship with any of the people who worked here during the construction?"

"If she did, I was not aware of it."

"I've heard that there's the possibility of having a memorial service for Brenda here?"

"Yes, Mrs. Lovell mentioned that this morning. I think the family has yet to make a decision. Brenda was not a member of our flock. But her family and friends would be welcome here. I don't think she was very religious, but Brenda was a very spiritual person. I had hoped that she would someday join us."

"Is there anything else you can tell us about her?"

"I'm sorry, I don't think so. Like I said, Ms. Manton was one of dozens of contractors on this job." After a long pause Gunne said, "Sheriff, if there isn't anything else, my calendar this morning is overfilled."

"Thank you for your time," said Ray. He dropped his card on the clear expanse of walnut. "If anything occurs to you that you think might help, give us a call."

20

~~~~

"What did you think?" asked Ray as he fastened his seat-belt.

"You should find out where he gets his hair cut. Nice suit, too. There was quite a contrast between Reverend Tim's red suspenders, flannel shirt, and jeans and Gunne's ensemble."

"Yes, that marriage isn't going to last long. Whatever Gunne needed from Tim, well..."

"And did you see the way he checked me out. I haven't been so carefully undressed in a long time. Glad I had clean underwear on."

"How do you feel about that? I suspect I'm about to get a blast of feminist anger."

Sue chuckled, started the engine. "Hey, he's handsome, beautifully dressed, and that fragrance—four notches above Old Spice and Brut. It's been a long, barren winter, Ray. Sometimes you've just got to enjoy whatever comes your way."

"We need to know a lot more about Rod Gunne."

"Did you see his diplomas? I think I memorized the pertinent data. When we get back to the office I'll see if they're real and do a complete background check." She looked over at Ray. "Where are we going?"

He opened a map and showed her their final destination. "When you come off the highway here, it's a seasonal road. I'm not sure how far we'll get. We'll walk or ski from that point."

"Molly's directions weren't too specific?"

"No, but she did say that the tree house was in a stand of oak over-looking this creek." He pointed with his finger. "So we make that our northern boundary and work back and forth. Hopefully we will locate the tree house, and maybe the elusive Tristan."

Sue turned and drove just off the highway, encountering deep drifts where she stopped. "I don't think we can get much farther without taking the chance of getting royally stuck." She looked over at Ray and asked, "Skis or snowshoes?"

"I'd like to do skis. But I think we've got to use snowshoes, the snow in the woods will be too deep."

Before they started on their trek, Ray opened a detailed map and laid it on the hood of the Jeep. "Let's go east down this trail. Right here," he pointed to a small squiggle in the map, "where the trail forks, we'll want to go north. It should be up in here somewhere, maybe two, two and a half miles. If we get to the stream, we'll follow it to the lake. I've got a compass, you've got a GPS. We've got lots of daylight left. Just a walk in the park on a lovely winter day."

"Sure," said Sue.

They took turns breaking trail, quietly moving through the deep snow and heavily forested, rolling terrain. Occasionally they would stop to rest and drink water, and then start off again. They stopped at the edge of a deep ravine that dropped down to a narrow, gently mur-muring stream in an otherwise silent landscape.

"Where to now?" asked Sue in a low voice.

Ray looked west. "Let's go down stream about fifty yards, and then work south a few hundred yards, then work back to the stream. I'll let you do the magic with the GPS."

He waited for Sue to set up the instrument and then followed her as they worked their way west and then south, their eyes searching the tree-tops in the old-growth oak, ash and pine forest for anything that looked unnatural.

"Nothing here," said Sue, catching her breath. "Let's go to the top of that ridgeline and work back toward the stream. And it's your turn to lead."

Ray slowly climbed the hill, carefully planting his poles, labori-ously pulling his snowshoes out of the deep snow, his legs beginning to scream with pain. He stopped at the top and waited for Sue, taking a moment to absorb the quiet beauty of the scene.

"Energy bar?" asked Sue, using her teeth to help tear open the wrapper.

"I'm okay," said Ray, taking the time to catch his breath and drink some more water.

After a few minutes they started off again. As they neared the ravine again, Ray slowed, then stopped. He pointed to the top of a massive, gnarled old oak.

"Eagle's nest?" asked Sue in a low voice.

"Look again."

They worked their way to the base of the tree.

"Very clever, really good work. And look, he's got a zip line rigged." Ray's eyes traced the course of the thin, narrow cable. He pointed to where the zip line was anchored on the other side of the stream. "There's his escape route, down across the ravine where he can jump into a kayak or canoe. Or maybe he keeps a mountain bike stashed somewhere when there is less snow." He pointed to an indentation in the snow. "And there's his path from the stream up to the tree. It's pretty drifted over. Looks like it hasn't been used in awhile."

"How does he get up there?"

"Interesting question. I imagine some kind of climbing technique."

"What do we do now?" Sue asked quietly.

"If he's as wily as Molly has suggested, and he's up there, he knows where we are. I guess we could try yelling up to him. Probably it should be you rather than me. He might relate better to a woman. Tell him we've come about Brenda, we need his help."

Sue moved back from the tree and cupping her hand near her mouth shouted toward the structure at the top of the tree. Then they stood and waited in silence, listening and watching for any sign of life from the carefully crafted dwelling.

"What do you think, should I try again?"

"Go ahead," said Ray.

Sue's second attempt didn't get any response either. "I could put a few rounds up there and see if any blood comes down. It would show up nice in the snow."

"Your humor is deteriorating. We better get going while we still have some daylight," said Ray. "Let's stop at my house and find something to eat."

"Okay, but I've got to pick up Simone from doggie daycare first."

21

S ue had been working at the computer for more than an hour when Ray returned to the office.

"Do you always have leftovers like that?" asked Sue as they settled in for an evening of work before Molly's arrival at 10:00.

"I thought I should feed you after that hike."

"And that tart was just amazing. Where do you get things like that?"

"It's a long story."

"And Simone really likes lamb. She may never eat dog food again." Sue looked over at the terrier curled tight and sleeping on an overstuffed chair in the corner of Ray's office.

"I feel guilty about not staying to help you clean up, but I did make good use of the time. I ran Rod Gunne's name on NCIC."

"And?"

"Nada. But Google is so wonderful. It may not list all of one's felonious records, but you can find almost everything else."

"Like?"

"How about an undergraduate degree from Northwestern in, let me get this right," Sue looked through some pages she had printed off, "radio/television/film media production and analysis. And for Rod Gunne's graduate work, an MBA with a specialization in concert management."

"How about theology, or demonology, or something related to his current career?"

"Wait, I'll get to that," said Sue. "Our reverend friend has already had a rather extraordinary career. Early on after his master's degree, he was managing the tours of well-known rock stars. Then he was recruited to manage a national tour for a prominent evangelist, and as the saying goes, he never looked back. Over the next several years he worked for some of the most successful televangelists in the country."

"Where did you find this stuff?" asked Ray. "Was it on his Website?"

"Lots of things get left on Websites long after they are current. So staff positions held by Rodney Gunne years ago are still out there on a variety of sites. So unless there's another Rod Gunne who attended the same schools as the Reverend at the same time, he's our man."

"So, how about his religious training?"

"He's certified by a small, fundamentalist sect in Michigan. He took an eight-week training course, and passed an exam and a required background and credit check. His name is on their list of accredited ministers. And his church, The Church for the Next Millennium, is duly registered in this state as an ecclesiastical corporation."

"You've done all that in an hour."

"There's more. Bring a chair over, I want you to see this," Sue moved to the right so Ray could get a good view on the big, flat-screen display.

"Look at the church's Website. It's spectacular. One of the best I've ever seen. They're using all the newest Web tools. You can stream his services live, but everything is also available as a Webcast that you can watch any time, anywhere in the world where you can get a high-speed connection. And for a modest contribution via your PayPal account, everything is available, including PDFs, CDs, and DVDs of sermons, even a personal prayer or inspirational thought from Reverend Gunne. And do you know what the beauty of all this is?"

"Go ahead."

"It's all electronic. Yes, he's got some development costs, but most of the content is delivered via the Web. He's not buying radio or TV time like the televangelists he worked for. He's taken it to the next level. This is brilliant. His costs are very limited, and his audience is worldwide. And if you want to come and personally worship at his church, you've got to look all over the Website to find its location."

"That's all well and good, Sue, but for all this technology to work for him, Gunne's got to be selling something people want."

"Here's his message," said Sue, pointing to the screen, *"God wants you to be wealthy.* This theme is repeated all over the Website, in the titles of sermons, Webcasts, and a whole array of things that are available for purchase. I can't say that I'm well versed in Christian theology, but this ain't your daddy's Methodist church. It looks like Gunne may be creating his own religious brand."

Ray gazed at the screen. "I think that message has been around for some time. But everything you're showing me suggests enormous sophistication at delivering his message. And I imagine that it would have special appeal during hard times. When I have time, I'd like to listen to some of his sermons, so I could better understand his appeal."

"There's one more thing you'll find interesting," said Sue. "I just want you to look at this piece of video. Watch when the focus moves from Gunne to the congregants. Look at those people. See anyone you know? Look at the great smiles, the wonderful grooming, and the way they are dressed. And they're all such good-looking people."

"Yes," agreed Ray. "Young, healthy, and vibrant. It doesn't look much like Reverend Tim's flock, does it?"

"No," agreed Sue. "It reminds me of the casino ads on TV, all the beautiful, happy people who are supposedly getting rich and having a wonderful time. You never see shots of the pensioners with their oxygen tanks sitting at the slots smoking and drinking."

"This is all fascinating, Sue. But do you see any connection to our case?"

"No, there's nothing obvious."

"Can you put some crime scene photos on the screen?"

"Sure. What are you looking for?"

"I'd like to see the area around the computer equipment. I want to look at the photos and see if her laptop was there."

"Give me your thought process on this," suggested Sue.

"We've touched on it before. If the assailant's original plan was to torch the house, they only had to incapacitate Manton. What was the motive? There was no evidence that the perp was beginning to ransack the house. Was there something on Manton's computer that they wanted to destroy? When they decided to get out of there fast, did they grab her laptop as well as her cell phone?"

Sue worked at the keyboard, and soon her screen and the large display mounted on the wall contained thumbnail images of the photos Sue took at the crime scene. "How about this one?" she asked. The photo showed the desk area with a keyboard and large Macintosh display. On the right side was a mouse pad and mouse. On the left was a small legal pad, a pen on top of it.

"Can you move the view farther to the right?" Ray asked.

Sue manipulated the view, showing the right side of the work surface. The area held only a tray, blank DVDs on a spindle, two packets of sticky notes, a round tin container with assorted pencils and pens and the ends of small white cables.

"Would you magnify those cables, one at a time?" asked Ray.

Sue pulled the connector on the first cable into sharp focus.

"That's an iPhone connector. Look at the one coming off my computer."

"Yes," agreed Sue. "And here's the second one. It leads to a transformer plugged into a wall outlet. So we know from Rod Gunne that she had a laptop and it wasn't there when I shot these photos—it was either somewhere else or the perp carried it away."

"So if the perp took it, why is it important?" asked Ray, thinking out loud. "They weren't stealing a computer, what could have been on the hard drive that was worth killing for?"

Sue pondered the question. "Photos, text, financial data, something very incriminating. It hardly seems likely, but could Manton have been involved in blackmailing someone?"

"That hardly seems to fit," agreed Ray, "but at this point we have to continue to be open to all possibilities. How about her car, did you check that?"

"Yes, other than a few reusable shopping bags near the rear hatch, it was empty."

"Did you happen to check the car for prints?"

"No. It was on the list of things I was going to do."

"And the phone records? Any word yet?"

"No, still waiting."

Ray suddenly felt very frustrated. He pulled himself out of the chair and moved to the whiteboard. "What do we know for sure?"

"The assailant knew about the plow, where it was kept, and how to drive it. And that he seems to have a fondness for fire," offered Sue.

"And there may be a missing laptop that might be somehow important. Lots of mays, mights, and somehows."

"Where do we go from here?"

"We've been here before, Sue. It's the long dark night of an investigation when you don't seem to be going anywhere. We just have to keep pushing forward, hoping we do something smart, or right, just get lucky, or get some help from the perp doing something really stupid.

"I think we need to push Molly harder," continued Ray, "and I still want to talk to Tristan Laird."

22

"We found Tristan's tree house, Molly. Your directions were right on," said Ray, trying to open the conversation on a positive note. "Have you been up there?"

"Sure, lots of times. It's especially nice in the winter. When the leaves are gone you get great views of Lake Michigan."

Ray noted that Molly seemed a bit less guarded. "How do you get up there, up into the tree house?" he asked.

"Tristan has a rope ladder."

"Is that what he uses?"

"No, that's just for us, Brenda and me. He uses some kind of climbing gear to get up, then tosses the ladder down for us."

"I don't know much about climbing, Molly. How does he do it?"

"He's got this nylon line with a weight on it that he shoots up over a branch with a slingshot. And he uses that line to pull a climbing rope. Then Tristan has this harness and stuff that he uses to get up near the top where he goes from branch to branch to get to the platform that holds his little house. He calls it his aerie."

"The aerie, what's it like?" asked Sue.

"It's really small, a rectangle. Two people will just fit if you sit at opposite ends or lie side by side. But it's neat. The interior is finished in pine. It looks like a cabin in a tiny sailboat. There are even a couple of porthole windows."

"Does it have heat?"

"He's got a little heater, propane, but the space is so small and so carefully insulated that it doesn't take much to keep the place warm. He says that he can heat it with a candle, and I think that's true."

"Molly, I checked his trailer on Sunday, and it didn't appear that he had been there in a long time. And I had the same impression yesterday when we were near the aerie," said Ray.

"He uses the trailer mostly in good weather, not that he stays there much, but he stores stuff there. And he really likes the tree house, especially in winter. But if something has spooked him, he's probably in hiding."

"And you've had no contact with him since Brenda was attacked?"

"True, I haven't seen him. We both took responsibility for Tristan, but Brenda was the main contact person, both with Tristan and his siblings. It wasn't like that in the beginning, but over the years that's just how it evolved."

"You've talked about this before, but would you tell us again the history of your relationship with Tristan."

"Well, like I probably said, we were in the same class at Leiston School. But the three of us were special friends. There was something a bit off with Tristan, but you know how kids are. They are so accepting. Years later Brenda said she thought Tristan had a form of autism, what did she call it. Starts with an "a" I think."

"Asperger's Syndrome?" asked Sue.

"That sounds right. But I don't think it's really such a big thing. And he went off to college and did okay. It was after college, that's when he got hurt. He fell when he was rock climbing and got a closed-head injury. And that's when he sorta wigged out totally and got just a bit too strange."

"How did you two become the people with special responsibility for Tristan?

"After he got out of the hospital and rehabilitation, he came up here. Over the years Brenda had gotten to know his family. But by then both of his parents were gone. He was a very late child. I remember when his parents came to Leiston for graduation, they were like the age of everyone else's grandparents." Molly paused, "Let's see, where was I?"

"Tristan ending up here," Ray prompted.

"Yes. I think he wanted to be near us. Brenda and I were his special friends. His brother and sister both live in Connecticut, they are much older, and I think they were just as happy not to have him move close to them."

"But they provide for him financially?"

"Yes, and I don't quite understand how it all works, if there's a trust fund from his parents or what, but things like the tax bills on the property or any kind of insurance payments are taken care of by a law office out east. And Brenda had a checking account where she could pay for things around here and give him cash when he needed some."

"Why not give him a debit card?"

"He's sort of spooked by banks. Like I keep telling you, Tristan isn't normal."

"But he was around a lot?"

"Yes, and you never know when he will pop up. We used to joke about him being our special stalker."

"But as far as you know he wasn't at Brenda's the night of the assault?"

"I don't think he was in the building. Although in the dead of winter he would sometimes crash with her on and off. He might have been in the woods nearby and seen all the activity, or he might have drifted through a day or two later. What you have to understand is that he's so sensitive. I mean, it's sort of spooky. He senses things that normal humans miss. Now he knows something awful has happened, and he's probably terrified."

"Molly, if he were around that evening, and he saw something, he could help us crack this case. Is there some way you could help us make contact with him?"

Molly looked thoughtful. "It's not as simple as that. He would find Brenda and me when he wanted something."

"Wouldn't he need cash? Won't he be coming to you soon?"

"I don't know. He can live a long time on his own. He can get by just on hunting and fishing. In the early winter, once we've got a good snowpack, he collects road kill, deer. He follows a county plow that comes through this one area that he watches before dawn, about four in the morning. He says most days he can find a fresh kill. He says the

meat is still warm when he butchers it, then he stashes it in the wild."
Molly looked over at Ray, "That's not illegal, is it?"

"There are some procedures the DNR would like people to follow,"
Ray answered.

Molly looked at her watch. "I've got to get logged in pretty soon,
guys."

"So you have no way of contacting him?"

"That's what I'm trying to tell you, Sheriff, and you just don't seem
to get it. I don't know where he is or how to get to him. If I did, I would
tell you. I want to find out who did this and get the bastard behind bars
or dead."

"One more question?" said Ray.

"Sure," Molly responded, getting to her feet.

"Did Brenda have a laptop computer?"

Molly was slow in responding. "I think so, I mean, everyone does."

"But you don't remember clearly seeing her with one."

"Like I said, they just seem to be part of everyone's life these days.
Is there anything else?' Molly asked, her tone bordering on hostility.

"No, I think that's all for now," said Ray. He followed her to the door
and closed it after her.

"Do we ever learn much from her?" asked Ray.

"Only what she wants us to know," said Sue. "But at least you got
a little affect this time. You need to get home and get some sleep. As
I remember it, you have a doctor's appointment tomorrow morning.
And I suspect that I should drive you to make it look as though you are
following the doctor's orders."

"I'm feeling fine, and I've got too much to do."

"As I remember it, your appointment is at eight."

"We've got to get our hands on Tristan."

"How do you propose to do that?" Sue asked.

"Well, we could go in fast on snowmobiles, have someone cover the
far end of the zip line, and send someone up there the way Tristan gets
up there."

"I can tell when you are really tired. Proposing to use a blitzkrieg
approach to go after someone. Didn't you just explain how a snowmobile would spook him? And how many times have you lectured me on

the insensitivity of law enforcement in dealing with mental patients? And you're grumpy again."

"What would you suggest?"

"We don't even know if he's there. So why don't we go out there again for a look. We will bring Brett Carty with us. He is a climber. Almost every weekend lately when he's off, he's up in the U.P. ice climbing at Pictured Rocks. Tomorrow, after your doctor's appointment and our interview with Elise Lovell, we'll go out there again."

"And for what it's worth, I'll write a note to Tristan explaining the situation—you get to edit it. Maybe we should even leave a cell phone."

"Cell phone," repeated Ray, "that's an interesting idea."

23

S ue had delivered Ray to his morning doctor's appointment a few
minutes before eight. He was settling into a chair in an examining
room after having his temperature and blood pressure taken by
Saul Feldman's nurse, when she told him that the doctor was running
late. Ray wanted to ask how Saul could be running late with the first
appointment of the day, but he held his tongue. And, in fact, Feldman
wasn't too late, but the appointment took longer than Ray had anticipated with Feldman explaining the results from tests, and presenting
several theories as to why Ray had blacked out. Feldman also gave him
a lecture on the need for more rest and a regular exercise program.

Ray had been back at his office for a few minutes when his secretary,
Jan, was at the door with Elise Lovell. Both women were redheads, but
Jan's hair was more the natural color, although she had been joking for
years that she had been aiding nature. Elise's hair, abundant, running
beyond her shoulders, was a rich dark red, not a natural color, but very
attractive against her complexion.

Elise was dressed in the same style as when Ray had first met her
during the investigation of Lynne Boyd's shooting. She was clad in
bright colors in what looked liked natural fabrics. Ray remembered
her jaunty style and keen intellect. He also remembered her great precision in characterizing Dirk Lowther. She had mirrored Ray's feelings for Lowther, emotions he knew he had never articulated with such
great accuracy.

Shortly after Elise was seated, Sue arrived with a pot of fresh coffee and pulled up a chair.

"Thank you for coming," said Ray, pouring coffee.

"I'm happy to help, Sheriff. Brenda was an amazing person. I can't imagine anyone wanting to harm her."

"Well, first, Ms. Lovell..."

"Please call me Elise," she interrupted. Ray noted her warm tone, her voice unusually deep for a woman. He also became aware of her perfume, subtle and very feminine.

"Elise," said Ray, starting again and feeling a bit uncomfortable. "Would you please provide us with some background on the nature of your friendship with Brenda Manton?"

"Certainly, I've known Brenda for years. I met her soon after my husband and I moved up here. I was just getting into spinning and dying back then. And Brenda was just beginning to move her art in that direction. She wasn't buying much locally then. She was looking for exotics in color and texture, and there was nothing like that produced here. When she found out about my background, she pushed me to develop my knowledge and skills in a new direction."

"Your background, would you talk about that?" asked Sue.

"I'm a chemist by training. I had a real interest in organic chemistry. Brenda got me to develop an expertise in natural fibers, especially wool, and in natural dyes. Initially I was just experimenting with materials I was using in my own knitting and weaving. Then I started sharing my yarns with friends, mostly trading out for wool and eggs and things. And then Brenda would come to me looking for specific colors. She would have these as part of a design, and she would generate the color on her computer and ask me if I could find something in nature that would generate that same hue."

"And you were able to?" asked Ray, filling a silence.

"Usually. I had a whole lot to learn about natural dyes and how they interact with different types of fibers. It turned out to be a lot of work, but it was incredibly interesting."

Ray was watching Elise's eyes as she talked. He wondered if they were really that green, or if their color was enhanced by her contact lenses.

"So you provided materials to her?"

"Yes."

"Was this just a business relationship, or did you develop a friend-ship as well?"

"Interesting question, Sheriff. I looked on Brenda as a friend, and I assumed she felt the same about me. That said, she was one of the most work-oriented people I've ever met. She was always on task. Before meeting Brenda I didn't fully appreciate what the term 'workaholic' meant. That really describes her. She was all about her art. Relation-ships were down the list a bit."

Ray glanced down at some notes he had made in preparation for the interview. "Did she ever mention fears about personal safety?"

"Never."

"Was Brenda in a relationship?" asked Sue.

"Not that I was aware of," Elise paused. "You know, I've never thought about it before, but I'm not sure we ever talked about men or relationships. Our conversations were focused on art and work."

"Did you visit Brenda at her home?"

"Yes, many times. She would show me early drafts of designs she was developing. She would have colors in mind and would want my counsel on whether it would be possible to produce yarns in those colors. She would go through this elaborate process of massaging her sketches to reflect what was possible with different dyes and fibers. Brenda was amazing, she was always pushing the boundaries of her art. That's why her work is so exceptional."

"When you visited her, was it just the two of you?"

"Yes, most of the time. Occasionally there was a strange character that she has some sort of custodial responsibility for."

"You're referring to Tristan?"

"Yes. I am enormously tolerant of eccentricity, but I found him a bit too weird."

"Was there something about his manner that you found threaten-ing?" asked Sue.

"No, it wasn't that. He just seemed creepy. He was always lurking about. He wouldn't talk to you, wouldn't meet your eyes. He made me uncomfortable."

"Did Brenda have a notebook computer?"

"Well, she did most of her work on a Mac, it was a big system, you know those tower kind of computers. But I think she had a notebook, too. In fact, I'm sure she did. I saw her showing some sketches to a client on a job recently."

"Where was that?" asked Ray.

"It's a church interior. She did a series of panels for them. It was a major piece of work."

"And you supplied the materials?"

"Many of them. I've really had to up my production to meet her needs for materials. And it's been very helpful for us. My husband's been working as a finish carpenter, and he's been getting very little work. Brenda's need for large quantities of specialty materials has been a real help to our family's economy."

"Let me ask you again. Brenda never shared with you that she was apprehensive about anything?"

"No." She paused for a long moment. "This is a long reach, she joked about the creep that plowed her out in the winter. Like he wanted to get some kind of trade out going for the plowing."

"So you went with her to visit The Church for the Next Millennium?"

"Yes, she said I had to see this place and meet the minister, Rod Gunne. I thought she was kidding about the name."

"What did you think?" asked Ray.

"Well, he's got a lot of money to spend on art, that's a good thing."

"Did he hustle you?" asked Sue.

"No."

"How about Brenda?"

"I don't think so. If he did, she never shared it with me. Is there anything else, Sheriff?"

"We're looking for someone who might have a motive to hurt Brenda Manton. Do you have anything that might help us?"

"I've told you what I know. I wish there were more. Other than that friend of hers, maybe the guy totally flipped out."

"Here is my card," said Sue, sliding it across the table.

Ray was making notes at his computer when Sue returned from walking Elise out.

"What did we learn?" he asked.

"Nothing startling."

"Yes," he responded.

"But I think you really like the crunchy granola type."

"What are you taking about?" asked Ray.

"She's a very pretty women, and I'm not sure I've ever seen you give anyone such rapt attention. And she knew she had it, too. It was fun for me to watch the dynamic."

"Is Brett ready for our expedition this afternoon?" Ray asked, changing the subject.

"He's totally geeked. I told him how Tristan gets his rope in place. Brett is bringing a throwing line and a slingshot."

"Everything else ready?"

"The things we talked about last night. I have a one-page letter soliciting Tristan's help and a cell phone programmed to call my phone. I have them sealed together in a weatherproof bag. If he's phobic about ATMs, he's probably afraid of cell phones, too."

"We do what we can," Ray responded. "Maybe we'll get lucky."

24

Ray, Sue, and Brett shared in transporting the climbing gear, each carrying part of it in a backpack. They started their trek into the deep forest in brilliant sunshine, a sharp contrast from a long string of gray days. Ray felt almost guilty to be buoyed by the weather.

They followed the path they made the day before, still clearly visible, although covered by a dusting of new snow. They moved quietly through the woods, no chatter between them, maintaining an interval of twenty yards.

Ray led the way, taking the first turn at breaking the trail. He settled into a comfortable rhythm with the snowshoes and poles moving forward in an almost mechanical precision. From time to time he would stop and listen—only the sound of wind high in the trees and the distant cawing of crows. As they neared their destination, a Coast Guard helicopter came over low and fast heading toward the big lake, the slapping of its blades and the roar of its engine shattering the near silent forest. Ray stood and waited for several minutes, until the sound was little more than a distant echo, then pushed forward again.

Ray was still several hundreds yard from their destination when he had a sense of foreboding. And afterward, when he ran the tape of his memories again, he couldn't find a hint of what put him on edge.

The air was crisp, the sky clear, and the snow a pristine blanket, individual crystals sparkling like diamonds on the rolling terrain. Ray stopped, signaling the others to do the same. He stood for several minutes, catching his breath and listening as he surveyed the landscape. Again, just the wind high in the trees, the conifers gently swaying, the maples and ash bare and still months away from new plumage, the oaks clinging to a few leathery-brown remnants of last year's foliage.

He slowly started forward again, his senses keen to any sound or movement. Ray was almost to the base of the tree when he first noticed the blood, a splattering pattern on the perimeter, a pooling at the center, crimson against white on the snow directly under the tree house. He stopped and gazed at the structure above. He pulled a pair of compact binoculars from an inner pocket and glassed the branches and underside of the nest. He could see the congealed liquid glistening on the branches, frozen droplets shaped by the gravitational pull, poised for their flight to earth.

He signaled for his colleagues to come forward.

"Oh my God!" said Sue as she stood at Ray's side and observed the scene.

"Looks like someone heard your joke."

Brett joined them and stood silently.

"What do we do now?" asked Sue.

"Got your camera?"

"Yes," Sue answered. She pulled off her pack and retrieved a camera from the interior. Ray and Brett held their positions as she carefully recorded the scene.

"Where do you think the shooter stood?"

"Here or a few feet back up the trail. The three of us probably marched over their tracks," Ray answered.

Ray turned to Brett, "Can you climb up there and see what's happened?"

"No problem."

"Anything we need to protect down here?" Ray asked Sue.

"No, I don't think so. We should search for brass, but we can do that later. Brett, take some rubber gloves. Once you're up there we'll figure out how to go forward without disturbing the scene."

Using a slingshot, it took three attempts before Brett successfully lobbed the weighted end of a thin nylon line over a large branch near the top of the tree. Using that line, he pulled his climbing rope, a two-inch thick piece of braided Manila, over the branch and back to earth.

He secured it to the base of a nearby tree, and then started toward the top of the tree, hands and feet working together in a skillfully coordinated exercise that quickly moved him to the top of the tree. He then climbed toward the structure, disappearing momentarily.

"You won't believe this," he shouted down.

"What did you find?"

"Come on up and take a look." Brett tossed down a rope ladder that nearly reached the ground.

"Is there room for both of us?" Ray asked.

"Yes, you just have to be careful."

"Why don't you go, Ray. I don't like heights."

Ray was startled. Sue always seemed fairly undaunted by physical challenges. He released the straps on his snowshoes and slowly ascended the ladder. Brett gave him a hand at the top and helped him onto the platform. Ray stood and viewed the surrounding country. From this perch he could see out onto the big lake and north to the dunes. He paused for a moment to take in the magnificent view. Then he knelt at Brett's side and looked through the open door of the skillfully crafted structure. The interior was lit by a series of windows, porthole-like in design. The sun reflected off the walls and ceiling of pine. Centered on the floor was a large flattened garbage bag, a blood-stained white tie at the end. Blood was splattered around the interior, on the walls and ceiling. Near the wall at the far end was a tightly rolled sleeping bag and a small stove with a hose running to a propane canister and a candle lantern, hydration bag, and a few pots. There was a small stack of paperback books at the far northeast corner. Ray had to control his curiosity, his need to climb through the gore to find out what Tristan had been reading.

Ray turned to Brett. "We need to get Sue and her camera up here."

As Ray descended the rope ladder, he could see Sue waiting near the base of the tree.

"What did you find?" she asked while he was about half way down.

"It's a crime scene," he said. "You've got to get up there with your camera. Brett will help you get on the platform. It's very secure up there. You'll have no problem.

Sue looked at him with a doubtful expression. He stood holding the ladder and he continued to keep it from swaying as she climbed.

Five minutes later she was on the ground, smiling. "Best crime scene I've ever done. No body. And it's incredible up there."

"What do you want me to do now?" Brett called from the aerie.

"Do you need anything else up there?" Ray asked Sue.

"I'd like to dig a few of the slugs out of the ceiling. We need to get some of the blood down, and we need a garbage bag to put the perforated one in. I'll have to go to my jeep to get the extra things, " Sue replied.

"We'll be back," Ray shouted up to Brett.

"Take your time," Brett responded.

25

"Well, this is a strange development," said Sue, as she came up for air from her container of sesame chicken.

"When the going gets weird, the weird turn pro," said Ray, pausing over tofu and vegetables.

"Who said that again?" questioned Sue.

"Richard Nixon."

"You're kidding," said Sue.

"Yes," he said, enjoying his own joke. "It was Hunter Thompson, but he was probably thinking about Nixon at the time."

"You don't think Laird could have heard me when I joked about putting a few rounds into his loft as a way of seeing if he was up there?"

"No. There was a fair amount of wind noise yesterday, and we were talking softly. And I don't think Tristan was up there. It was more about our trail in and out."

"I don't think I quite follow."

"Trying to put together what Molly's been telling us. Let's go with the assumption that Tristan was somewhere near Brenda's place on the night of the attack. And let's also assume that Tristan saw the assailant and vice versa. Tristan is now on the run, but we assume he's still in the area. Sunday I hiked into his place, leaving tracks. Yesterday we checked out the tree house. What's he thinking, especially if he's reasonably fearful?

"Again, accepting Molly's view of his suspicious nature, he's thinking that someone is out to kill him too.

"And Molly told us that he's mostly nocturnal and that he roams his territory like a wild animal. We have to assume that he knows that someone checked out his trailer and then his tree house. He also knows that while few people would have the skills to get access to his tree house, they'd have no trouble killing him by pumping a dozen rounds into the place. And if the shooter stood around for a few minutes and waited for some blood to start seeping out of the place, they would have been convinced they killed Tristan."

"And this could have worked to his advantage in several ways," said Sue, starting to run with Ray's thinking. "It would get the hunter off his back, and on the off chance that he might be out there plotting some kind of revenge or an offensive move, his adversary would be clueless." Sue stirred her food with a plastic fork, finally spearing a piece of chicken. "How do we get our hands on him?" she asked, before popping the morsel into her mouth.

"You're usually the good one at generating novel ideas."

"I don't know, Ray, I've just been in a funk lately. We're so short staffed and the workload's been so high all fall and winter." Sue paused, her tone changed. "And I don't have much life outside of the job. When I do get home, I just crash. I haven't been going to my yoga class or hanging out with my friends. And as for men, well," Sue paused midsentence. "But the sun today was terrific. Maybe it's the grayness this time of year, that's what gets to me, the lack of sun for weeks at a time."

"Yes, it gets to me, too. And it's been a difficult period for both of us." Ray let his comment hang for a while, focused on his food. "How do we get to Tristan?"

"Well, our cell phone idea was a flop. I don't think he's planning on going back to his aerie anytime in the near future," said Sue, closing her Styrofoam container and breaking the seal on a bottle of Diet Coke, pausing briefly, then twisting the cap off. "We could tweet him," she suggested with a wry smile.

"I think at this point we can't do much more about Tristan other than getting Molly's full cooperation. If he contacts her, and she feels like cooperating with us, maybe she can bring him in. I'm afraid if we pursue him much more, he'll just go deeper to ground."

"The blood?"

"I've got a sample on the way to the State Police lab. Any bets?"

"I imagine he just collected another road kill. A deer would give him a pretty good quantity of blood."

"What if it was human?" asked Sue.

"That would be an interesting turn of events," said Ray coming to his feet and gathering up the food container and coffee cup. "Let's hope things don't become even more complex."

26

It was only a few minutes after seven when Ray got home, but he was feeling weary. He wished that it were late enough to just call it a day and go to bed, but if he allowed himself to get to sleep early, he knew that he would be wide awake at three.

He carefully arranged kindling in the fireplace and got a fire going. Then he boiled some water and made a pot of chamomile tea. He was settling down to read a copy of a new memoir by a poet that his local bookseller had recommended when headlights flashed across the window facing the drive. Seconds later came the sound of a car door being slammed shut. Ray unlocked and opened the front door. Hannah Jeffers entered in ski clothing.

"Could I talk you into hitting the slopes with me for a couple of hours this evening?" she asked, pulling off a knit hat.

"I haven't been out yet this season. I bought a pass in June or July and haven't even picked it up." Ray looked at his watch. "By the time I find everything, and we drive there, the lift operators would be yelling last run. I've just made a pot of herbal tea, would you like a cup before you hit the slopes?"

"Are you sure I'm not imposing?"

"No, I'm happy to have the company."

Ray moved the teapot to the kitchen table, and retrieved cups and saucers from a cupboard. He set these on the table, going back for spoons and a jar of local honey.

"I saw Saul this morning," he said as he settled across from Hannah.

"How did that go?" she asked.

"The usual. I'm supposed to get more sleep, eliminate stress from my life, lose ten pounds, and yada yada yada."

"Do you smoke?" she asked.

"No. Quit a long time ago."

"Too bad."

"Why's that?"

"There are so many great diseases connected with smoking. It gives us a terrific chance to jazz up a physician/patient lecture. Excessive alcohol and abusing prescription drugs are also good triggers. And then there's meth, crack and..."

"Do you see many of those?"

"No, not up here. Not like Detroit. Occasionally in the ER we see some serious overdoses. I gather the problem in this area is more with the abuse of prescription drugs. In the doctors' lounge I hear stories about people shopping physicians looking for soft touches. You probably know more about it than I do."

"It's part of the environment now. From time to time we'll get a flurry of activity and make some arrests. Then things will quiet down for a while, but it's always going on." Ray filled the cups and pushed the bottle of honey toward Hannah. "That's local honey, star thistle, supposed to help your immune system with hay fever or something."

"Does it?"

"Who knows," said Ray. "But it tastes good, especially in tea. How did you end up in medicine?"

"My father was a surgeon, so was my grandfather. It just seemed the thing to do."

"Do you have siblings?"

"No, I was an only child. How about you?"

"Same," said Ray.

"How did you end up in the military?" Ray asked

"The army paid for a big part of my medical education. My military service time was paying back that obligation and getting additional training and experience. I was actually geeked up about going into a combat zone. I was going to get a whole lot of experience dealing with traumatic injuries."

"How did that go?"

"I'm a skilled thoracic surgeon, good at cracking chests and dealing with heart problems and traumatic injuries," she paused for a long time. "I came to the military with previous experience in big city ERs where you think you're in a war zone much of the time. I was confident that I had the kind of professional detachment to get through it, but I was wrong. I got worn down," she said as she stirred honey into her tea.

"It's confronting of horrific injuries day after day, the IEDs. I hate those fucking things. The blast damage, the tearing wounds from the shrapnel. And these kids, they're so young, many of them, eighteen, nineteen, twenty. I was often up to my elbows in blood, trying to pull off another miracle. But lots of time there was just too much damage. I'd think about their lives, everything that had happened to get them to this point and how if I could get them through it...." Hannah sipped her tea. "You get ground down. Every time you hear the choppers you know you're going to confront something awful. And when you aren't working, you are a prisoner in this little compound in the Green Zone. It was a special kind of hell.

"My father was a surgeon in Vietnam," she continued, "but he never talked about it. He was an alcoholic. I don't know what part the war might have played in that. He died young, on the golf course, massive coronary. My grandfather was a flight surgeon in World War II. He was stationed in England with a bomber group. He was a tough guy, practiced medicine until he was almost eighty. He came back from the war hating politicians. I don't think he ever voted again."

"So where are you?" Ray asked.

"I don't know. I got some counseling when I left Baghdad and was assigned to Landstuhl and did some more when I got back to the D.C. area. Then I went up to Boston for a special program. The military has finally figured out that women get PTSD, too. For a while I was drinking too much, I worried about that a lot. I thought it might be in my genes. I think I'm past that, the drinking. I just need to keep myself busy with work and exercise. I need to physically exhaust myself daily with running or skiing or kayaking or something."

"What brought you to this area?" Ray asked.

"My grandparents had a place on Glen Lake. I came up north as a kid, lots of good memories. And there was a guy up here, someone I knew in medical school."

"What happened with him?"

"People change. When we were sort of a couple in medical school, he was so idealistic. He went into family medicine and later opened West Shore Village Clinic up here. When we hooked up again he was all upset about how much, or I guess I should say, how little money he was making. And then he got involved in this church. I mean, he's this smart sophisticated man and he seemed totally taken in by this minister with strange beliefs about Jesus wanting everyone to be rich. He dragged me along to church a few times. It was just weird. It's a new church of some sort, modern, feels like a sports bar on the interior, screens all over. The minister preaching at you from all directions interspersed with some pretty good rock and roll. I mean, I'm no expert on Christian theology or anything, but it just seemed like the minister was pushing a religion of materialism. It felt like a real slick sales meeting."

"Did you meet the minister?"

"Oh yeah, Bob wanted me to get to know this guy, Rod Gunne. We had dinner with him one night at this little French restaurant. I mean, Bob is really cheap, but he happily picks up this enormous tab. The minister was there with some real babe, but he spent most of the evening hitting on me. Bob didn't seem to notice. That was the end. I told him that evening when he was driving me back to my apartment that I didn't think we were on the same wave-length. Other than running into him at the hospital occasionally, I haven't seen him since."

27

Ray brought the phone to his ear and identified himself. He listened for a long moment and then asked, "Is there anyone available to check it out?"

"Okay," he finally said. "Keep checking back with the mother. Instruct her to call you if the kids appear. And I'd like you to call the Last Chance, talk to Jack. If Henry is there, find out if his kids are with him and tell Jack to hold onto him until I arrive. Call me back as soon as you know that he's there. I'll be on my way in a few minutes." Ray ended the call.

"What's going on?" Hannah asked.

"A couple of young kids, I think they are five and seven now, were spending the day with their father. He was supposed to have them home by six. The kids never arrived and their mother can't reach the father. The mother has a tendency toward hysteria, but given the history of her relationship with this man, I understand completely. He's an irresponsible drunk."

"So what are you going to do?"

"When he's not working, he's usually drinking at the Last Chance. If the kids are with him, I'll take them home. If they're not, I need to find out where they are."

"Any chance I could tag along?"

Ray thought about her request for a long moment. "Sure. What do you have on your feet?"

"Hiking boots."

"Do you have your snowshoes with you?"

"Everything is in my rolling toy chest."

"Bring them, just in case."

They were just getting into Ray's car when he got a second call from County Dispatch. After switching off the phone, he said to Hannah, "As expected, the father is at the Last Chance doing shots of Jim Beam washed down with Bud Light."

Before entering the bar, Ray walked around Travis Henry's dilapidated Dodge pickup, shining his flashlight into the window on the off chance that Travis might have left his children out there. All he could see was litter: soiled clothing, rusting tools, empty fast food and coffee containers, and crushed beer cans.

As Ray entered the Last Chance, Jack, the owner and bartender, now in his eighties, motioned with his head toward the far end of the bar. Ray approached the man, Hannah hanging back and observing. He climbed on to the stool next to Travis Henry, who was slouched over an empty shot glass, a half-empty shell of beer near his left hand.

"Hi, Travis. How you doing tonight?" asked Ray.

Henry didn't move, his eyes fixed on an empty pack of Marlboros, the lid torn away.

Ray waited.

"Sheriff," Travis finally mumbled, without changing his focus.

"Got a call from Phoebe. She's worried about the kids."

"I took 'em back. Maybe a little late. I took 'em back."

"Back to the house, back to Phoebe's house?"

"I dropped them off at Platte Line Rd. Let them walk home. I didn't want to talk to the bitch."

"Where on Platte Line?"

"Off twenty-two."

"Travis, that's a seasonal road. It's not plowed. And it's got to be more than a couple of miles."

"Like I said, I didn't want no argument. I was late. And the road's not that bad. Snowmobiles have been flattening it."

"How were the kids dressed?"

"Winter stuff, coats, hats, boots. Probably home by now."

Ray slid off the stool and headed for the door, Hannah followed. She listened to his side of the phone conversation after climbing into the passenger seat.

"Get someone down here, I want Henry stopped as soon as he pulls onto the highway. Any word on the children?" Ray listened to the response. "I'll do a quick sweep. I may need to have you organize a lot of help. I'll be in touch."

"What's happening?" Hannah asked.

"No sign of the kids. The mother's becoming increasingly hysterical. Let's do a quick sweep and see if we can find them."

Ray switched on the overhead flashers and hit the accelerator as soon as his vehicle was on the dry pavement of the highway.

"You know this guy?" asked Hannah.

"He's always on the radar."

"How so?"

"He's a drunk. He's always in some sort of trouble. Minor stuff."

"Why don't you take away his license?"

Ray chuckled. "I don't know if Travis ever had one to take away." He thought about his response a bit. "Probably had one once, years ago."

"Why isn't he in jail?"

"He's been our guest from time to time. And when he isn't drinking, he's not such a bad guy. He just can't stay away from the booze."

"How does he survive?" Hannah asked.

"He does drywall and plaster. He works for one of the high-end builders who swears that there is no one around that is as good as Travis. His boss will be in tomorrow morning bailing him out."

"Isn't there anything that you can do?"

"It's a catch-22. He makes good money, pays child support and provides the kids with health insurance. If he gets locked up for a long time, that all goes away. It's a real problem for the prosecutor."

Ray slowed and turned onto an unplowed road, his vehicle coming to a halt in the deep snow. With snowshoes and poles, they started down the road, forests on one side, long-abandoned farm fields with random clusters of scraggy cedar on the other. The center of the road had been packed down by snowmobile traffic, off that track the snow was several feet deep, sometimes more, in areas where drifts had formed.

Ray followed the snowmobile track, checking the sides of the road for any evidence that the children had veered off in another direction. The stark white glow of Ray's LED headlamp reflected eerily off the crusted snow. Occasionally he would stop and shout the children's names, then wait for a response before starting off again.

"Are we getting close?" Hannah asked, following Ray closely.

He stopped and checked his watch. "We're more than half way," he answered.

"Emily, Zack," he shouted, then waited. The snow-covered landscape was a dull gray under the heavy cloud cover. In the far distance the silence of the winter night was broken by the sudden scream of a snowmobile engine. After it faded away Ray yelled again. They stood and waited. "Did you hear that?"

"Just barely," said Hannah. "Was that a child or something else?"

With an increased sense of urgency, Ray moved forward again, almost a jog on the heavily packed snow. He stopped and yelled again. This time the response was clear, the voice of a child.

He found and then followed a path off the trail into the woods. A small girl, waist deep in snow, was standing in the skirt of a tall pine. "We're here," she shouted.

"Where's your brother?" Ray asked as he approached her.

"He's here in our fort," she said, pointing to an opening in the branches that extended down into the snow.

Ray dropped to his knees, his lamp lighting the interior of the natural shelter. He could see Zack curled up near the trunk of the tree looking chilled and frightened.

"Why did you stop here? Why didn't you go home?" he asked.

"Zack lost a boot and his sock in the snow. He didn't tell me when it happened. When he started crying I went back to look, but I couldn't find them. I remembered this place. We play here in the summer. I put my mitten on his foot. I thought mom would come and find us. She's been here before."

Ray pulled off his backpack and retrieved a blanket from the interior. "Come here, Zack," he instructed. Then he wrapped the frail, frightened child in fleece. Turning to Emily, he asked, "Do you think you can walk home, or do you want my friend to help you?"

"I'm okay," said Emily, "but I was starting to get awful cold."

Ray pulled a second fleece blanket from the pack and wrapped it around her shoulders. He secured his poles to the pack, pulled it on, and then picked up Zack, cradling him in his arms.

"Come on, Emily, let's get your little brother home."

In less than twenty minutes they were in the kitchen of the old farmhouse. Hannah Jeffers checked the children for possible injuries from their extended exposure to the cold while Ray worked to calm their mother.

By the time they left, the children were in a warm bath, Hannah assuring Phoebe that she could find no medical problems, and that a bath and a good night's sleep was the best treatment at the moment.

"Do you want to snowshoe back to the car, or should I have someone come and get us?"

"Snowshoe," said Hannah, "If you're okay with that."

"Yes," said Ray, although he was feeling weary. The clouds had cleared and the cold glow of the moon reflected off the snow. They switched off their headlamps and retraced their path by moonlight in the cold winter night.

28

Ray was keying his report on Travis Henry when Sue Lawrence rolled her acrylic nails at the side of his open door.

"Good morning," he said looking in her direction. "What's up?"

"I have a woman here who wants to file a missing persons report. I think you'll be interested in her story."

"How so?"

"She's an expat, she's been living in China. She's back in the States for a few months and came up here to check on her parents. She says she's not close with them, especially her father, but they are getting quite elderly and she thought she should drop in on them."

"And they've gone missing?"

"Well, it's more than that," said Sue, warming to the story. "As she describes it, her parents live in a walled compound, says her father is a security freak. They have a large home on a bluff overlooking the big lake. The place is surrounded by a high fence and gated drive. She went to visit them last evening, thought she would surprise them. The gate was open, she rang the doorbell and...."

"Come on, Sue, don't keep me in suspense."

"A total stranger answered the door, identified himself as Rod Gunne. Seems he's living there. Says her parents gave him the use of their home."

"A couple of days ago I had never heard of Rod Gunne. Now his name just keeps popping up in almost every conversation."

"It's kinda weird, isn't it. Do you have time to hear her story?"

"Please bring her in. This should be very interesting."

When Ray returned to his office with a fresh flask of coffee and some clean mugs, Sue was waiting, standing beside a slight, delicate woman who appeared to be in her late thirties or early forties.

"Sheriff Elkins, this is Stephanie Janzen."

Ray took her hand, noting that her frail figure belied her obvious strength.

"Please have a seat," said Ray, directing her to a chair at the conference table. "Coffee?"

"Please."

Ray filled a mug and passed it to her, sliding a small tray of sugar and creamer in her direction.

"Where would you like me to start?" Janzen asked, stirring her coffee with a plastic spoon.

"At the beginning, please," said Ray, carefully studying her delicate facial features: large sensitive eyes, skillfully styled hair.

"Well, as I told the detective here," she motioned toward Sue, "I'm back in the States for a month. I live in China."

"How long have you been in China and when did you last see your parents?"

"I've been working abroad since graduate school, mostly in Asia. I've been in mainland China almost twelve years."

"What do you do?" asked Ray.

"I'm a translator and technical writer, although now I'm mostly doing management. I very seldom come back to the States. When I go on holiday I usually go some place in Asia or Europe."

"But this time you came to visit your parents?"

"Well, actually, that had not been my plan. I've been having a few health issues, and my employer wanted me to go to Mayo Clinic, they have an excellent executive medical program. After my checkup I had a few extra days, so I thought I'd run over here and see how they are doing. My parents, they're not getting any younger, and I thought I should make one more attempt at reconnecting."

"I'm not quite following," said Ray.

"We've been alienated, my father and I, since I was a teenager. My mother has been dead for years, she passed away when I was still in college. He remarried soon after. The new wife, Vera, seems nice enough, but I hardly know her."

"Would you give me your father's and stepmother's names, please?"

"Russell and Vera Janzen."

"So continue with your story. You arrived yesterday and..."

"Yes, it was late afternoon. I'd rented a car at the airport and drove out to their house."

"And you hadn't called or anything?"

"No, I thought it was better to just arrive. I didn't want to give him a chance to reflect on old enmities."

"When did you last have contact with your father?" Ray asked.

"It's been a number of years. Like I said, we've been alienated."

"Continue with your story, please."

"I drove out to the house, and I was actually quite surprised to find the security gate on his road open. I knocked on the door and was greeted by this total stranger who identified himself as Reverend Gunne. He invited me in; he was entertaining a couple of women, it looked like they were having drinks. I explained who I was and told him I was there to visit my parents.

"Gunne told me that my parents had given him the use of their house for the winter and that they were in Mexico and last he heard planning to stay there until June."

"And then what happened?"

"I thanked him and left. I went back into Traverse City and got a hotel room. I had a hard time sleeping. There is something so wrong here."

"Ms. Janzen, it's not unusual for summer residents to rent out or allow others to use their summer homes."

"You don't understand, Sheriff. My father is a selfish, suspicious old bastard. He's never given anything away in his life. The last thing in the world he would do is let someone use his house. Just let me tell you how crazy he is. He's got this big old RV, it's a Bluebird. When he and Vera were going on a trip, they would move into the RV. He'd set the alarm system in the house, and then they would stay in the RV for a few days. My father wouldn't leave until he was convinced that everything was working properly. Then he'd chain and lock the front gate before he drove away."

"If he's not there, where else could your father be? Perhaps he is in Mexico. Do you have any way of contacting him, cell phone, Internet?"

"My father would never go Mexico. He's xenophobic, doesn't like people who don't speak English, let alone have a different skin tone."

"Do you have siblings or relatives who might have recently had contact with your father or his wife?"

"I'm an only child. Vera never had children. And I don't think my father has been in touch with relatives for decades. He had an older brother, I don't know if he's still living."

"How about neighbors, friends..."

"If they have friends, I wouldn't know. Same with neighbors. What I'm trying to tell you is that he's absolutely misanthropic."

"Has your father ever disappeared before?"

"Not that I know of."

"And, again, when did you last see your father? Please be as specific as possible."

Stephanie remained silent for a minute, and finally said, "I'm not quite sure, it's been six or seven years."

"Have you communicated with him by phone, letters, e mail."

"No, but I don't think that's of any significance here. There are strange people in my father's house, and I want you to investigate this immediately. What do I have to do to make this missing persons thing official?"

"Ms. Janzen, let me give you a couple of scenarios for what we normally consider a missing person. For example, a woman talks to her elderly father on the phone around noon. Later that day after work she stops by to see him and drop off some groceries that he has requested. When she gets to his home she find the front door wide open; it's winter. She checks with the neighbors and no one has seen him. His wallet and keys are on the kitchen table. Here's another example, a college girl who lives with her parents goes on a date. She tells them she's going to a concert and will be very late. The next morning they find that she has not returned. About noon they try her cell phone. She doesn't answer. By six in the evening they have heard nothing from her, which is totally out of character.

"In both cases you will note that the disappearances are totally out of character with the persons' normal behavior...."

"Yes, but...."

"You've told me that you have not had any contact with your father in years. When you suddenly pop in, he's not there. There's nothing to suggest that something untoward has happened to him or that he and your stepmother have gone missing."

"You know what really amazes me," Janzen said in a vituperative tone, "petty bureaucrats worldwide are all cut from the same cloth. You all seem determined to do as little as you can. And no imagination, none of you."

Without losing his aplomb, Ray responded. "Detective Lawrence will ask you for some additional information about your father and get your contact information. We will make some inquiries."

Ray came to his feet and offered his hand.

Janzen glared at him momentarily, and then followed Sue out of his office.

Ray was working through a long list of unanswered emails when Sue appeared at his door.

"When the going gets weird, the weird get going," she said with a wry smile.

"Who are you quoting?" asked Ray.

"Richard Nixon, or someone like that. How about lunch? I'll buy. I'll even go to the Health Hut."

"You're on. And after that, I want to visit Ben Reilly, and I want you with me. Let's see how he's doing now that he's out of the hospital."

29

Ray was settled into the passenger seat as Sue drove north toward Ben Reilly's home. Again he was struck by how much more of the countryside he was able to observe when he didn't have to have his eyes glued to the road. He was continually surprised to see things for the first time even though he had traveled these roads for decades.

The bright sun glistened off the rolling, snow-covered fields with their neat rows of carefully pruned fruit trees and grapevines. When spring arrived, there would be a flurry of activity on the farms, but now things were still suspended in winter's grip.

In contrast to the coastal areas and the resort lakes, much of the interior of Cedar County had changed very little over the years. Many of the original houses and barns built after the lumber had been cut more than a hundred years before still remained. Ray could see the outline of cracked fieldstones in the foundations of the barns. And although most of the farmhouses had gone through numerous remodels with many additions, he could usually identify the outline of the original structure.

This was the area and these were the people with whom he'd grown up. His parents' farm, inherited from his mother's family, was small and the land was of poor quality, much of it low and swampy. Although Ray's father did some farming, the majority of the family's modest income came from his father's work as a handyman and jack-of-all-trades.

But Ray remembered the many years when the neighboring farms lost their cherry or apple crops to a late frost, or the corn harvest failed due to lack of rain. Farming in the region was always a gamble, some years providing a bountiful harvest, other years returning little more than disappointment and debt for months of backbreaking work.

"Are we getting close?" asked Sue, depending on Ray for directions.

"Just over that hill and down about halfway. The drive is on the left."

Sue parked in a large plowed area between the house and barn near the back entrance to the house. Maureen, Ben's wife was at the door to greet them, pushing the storm door open as they approached. She led them through the kitchen to the family room, part of an addition they had added to the old farmhouse when their children were young.

Ben was in a large overstuffed chair, his casted right foot resting on an ottoman. He was holding an eBook reader in his right hand. He set it in his lap and high-fived Ray, then Sue.

"How are you feeling?" asked Ray.

"Still a little sore," Ben responded, "and a bit caged." He lifted his left arm, also wrapped in a plaster cast.

"How long will you be sporting those?" asked Ray.

"Whatever it is, it's too long," Ben answered.

"The orthopedist said probably about six weeks," said Maureen, "depending on how he does and how good of a patient he is. So, Ray, tell him to behave."

"The physical therapist was here this morning," said Ben.

"Cute redhead," added Maureen. "I've never seen him so cooperative. Can I get you two coffee or tea?"

"I'm good," said Ray.

"Me, too," responded Sue.

"So tell me about the case. What do you know?" asked Ben.

"At this point it's more what we don't know," said Ray. Then he and Sue took turns providing a narrative of the investigation from the point where Ben was injured to Stephanie Janzen's story of her parents' alleged disappearance and Rod Gunne taking up residence in their manse.

"Where is this place," asked Ben, "this 'manse'?"

"It's somewhere south of Crescent Cove. You know the area, lots of very private homes and gated drives. You can't see much from the road," said Sue.

"Did you ever hear of Russell Janzen?"

"No, never on my radar. Remember a few years ago when we had a burglary on some new construction in that area? A hundred thousand dollars in cabinets went missing."

"Yes," said Sue. "Another one of America's unsolved mysteries. The place was very isolated, especially in February, and the contractor had really lax security. I remember he said something like, 'This is God's country. I've never lost anything before.'"

"Richard Kinver," said Ray, moving the conversation in a new direction. "He owned the plow that crashed into us. It was found the next morning. It had been torched. He had reported it stolen, and he seems to have a solid alibi. What do you know about Kinver?"

"I'm sure you know the family has been around forever?"

"Yes," said Ray. "I was just wondering if you ever had any run-ins with Richard."

"When I was first up here, he was just a teenager. He was a wild kid, lots of drinking, wrecked cars, fights."

"This all happened when he was a minor?" asked Ray.

"Minor and beyond," answered Ben. "His grandfather was still on the county board. And you've heard lots about how Sheriff Orville ran the department. Young Richard was part of Orville's friends and family protection plan. He took care of tickets and made sure minor offenses never got to the prosecutor." Ben chuckled. "Old Orville had lots of friends. He never had any trouble getting reelected."

"Anything more than wild oats?" probed Ray.

"The wild oats were pretty wild. And his first wife, tiny woman, red hair like Sue's. Wow, was she fiery. They were just kids, maybe twenty. I was out there several times on domestics. He was a mean drunk, but she was so much smarter than him."

"Would there be any record of this?" asked Sue.

"Friends and family," said Ben. "Lots of things were never documented."

"Do you remember her name?" asked Ray.

"Just her married name. As I remember it, the first name was Jill or Jen or Jean. They only made it a year or two. Later I heard that she moved out of state to go to college."

"Anything else we should know about Richard Kinver?" asked Sue.

"I recall there were some problems early in his second marriage too, years ago. Maybe he grew out of wife beating."

"Anything else?" asked Ray.

"He had good parents, and his grandfather was a real character. The gene pool must have been running dry when Richard came along. I've always found him arrogant and stupid, not a winning combination."

"One more thing, Ben, do you remember if Richard was ever connected to suspicious fires?"

"Not that I can think of." He paused and looked reflective. "Now that I think about it, he was connected to a fire, but it wasn't suspicious. He freely admitted setting it. The Kinvers had a pile of old tires out at their equipment yard. His father told him to get rid of them and Richard decided the easiest way to accomplish this was just to pour kerosene on them and burn them. The fire got out of control and it looked like it might spread to the surrounding forest. So Richard drives over to the township fire hall and comes back with the fire truck. Eventually some of the other volunteer firefighters showed up, and they got the blaze under control. Now here's the kicker, Richard puts in for his fire pay, but he's the one that started it. There was a story in the Weekly Standard and then some letters to the editor. But you know how those things go. In a few weeks most everybody had forgotten about it."

"Don't you think you should tell Ray about what we've been discussing," said Maureen, who had been sitting quietly at Ben's side.

"I don't know what we've decided for sure," he responded.

"I think we have," said Maureen. She looked straight at Ray and began, "Ben's got more than enough years in to retire. We've been talking it over. It seems this might be a good time. Our youngest, Jamie, will be finally graduating at the end of April. So we got all the kids through college. And there is a lot to do around here now that Ben's vineyard is starting to mature and the new orchards are coming into production." Maureen paused for a long moment, she appeared to Ray to be on the edge of tears. "Ben's getting hurt, this was an important message. And we're taking note."

After a long silence, Ray asked, "When do you think you would like to retire?"

"I'm still getting used to the idea," Ben responded. "I was told by one of the doctors that I probably wouldn't be able to return to work for at least six to eight weeks. It will be almost spring by then, lots to do around here."

Ray took a deep breath, exhaling slowly. "It's hard for me to think about the department without you, but I can understand your thinking. Once you've decided for sure, let me know how I can help." Ray looked over at Sue. "I think we should be going,"

They said their goodbyes to Ben, and Maureen walked them to the door. She followed Ray outside. "I know it will be hard for Ben to retire, he loves police work. But I want to have him to grow old with. It would be the best thing for both of us."

"I understand," said Ray.

Maureen gave him a quick hug, then turned toward the house.

30

Ray set the four bags of groceries on the kitchen counter and started unpacking them. As he put away the food he reflected on the events that had taken place since the assault on Brenda Manton. He thought about the flurry of activity that had absorbed his and Sue's time and energy in the past week. "Just flailing around," he said out loud, giving voice to his frustration at the lack of focus in the investigation.

He opened the refrigerator and looked at the array of wilted and sagging produce. Moving the trash container next to the door, he tossed all the rotting and soured food into the garbage, and in a second pass removed anything else that was slightly suspect. After cinching the ties on the plastic bag and carrying it to the garage, he put away the fresh produce, fruit, milk, yogurt, and eggs.

Ray turned his attention to making dinner, an omelet with some sharp Vermont cheddar, and a salad. He cut a few pieces from a fresh baguette and poured some olive oil in a ramekin for dipping. He thought about opening a bottle of wine, but settled on soda water. Once everything was ready, he sat down at the kitchen table.

His cell phone rang as he lingered over a *New Yorker* article after completing his meal. Sarah's face appeared on the phone's display.

"Hello, friend," he said after unlocking the phone.

"Hey, how are you?"

"I'm good. How's life?" he asked.

"Oh, Ray, it is so different. I'm used to being surrounded by adolescent drama and chaos. It is so quiet at the law office, all those people and so little noise. Everything happens behind closed doors, and the voices in the hallways always seem to be muted. But I'm starting to learn the lay of the land."

"Any surprises?" he asked.

"Not really. I did this kind of work in Detroit before coming to Leiston. It's just a different cast of characters and a much more affluent client base. And the city is great. I walked through a few galleries at the Art Institute during my lunch break today. I think I'm really a city girl at heart."

"Any chance of you coming up for the weekend?"

"I'm way too busy, Ray. I'll be working Saturdays until I get things under control. How about you coming to Chicago sometime?"

"I'm right in the middle of a murder investigation…"

"I think that's part of our problem, you're always in the middle of something. Listen, I've got to run. I'm going to the Lyric, and I've got to get ready."

"What are you going to see?" asked Ray, responding to the surface information, while thinking about the subtext.

"I don't know, and I've really got to run. I'll call you soon."

"Take care," he said, suddenly aware that she had switched off before the words were out of his mouth.

You are going to the opera, but you don't know what you are going to see. The thought bumped around in his brain, generating a rather obvious conclusion. It was followed by *I think I'm a city girl at heart.*

Ray mused about his relationship with Sarah. Little more than four or five months had passed since he had first met her, one of the most intense periods of his life. They had quickly developed a bond, perhaps more as a result of their mutual grief and loss. And when he was wounded, she was at his bedside. He had become enamored with her warmth and charm. He loved walking the beach with her and sharing quiet dinners. It was beginning to seep in that whatever they had was quickly vanishing.

As Ray sat at the table mulling over the contents of their phone conversation, he realized that they had never talked about the future. Everything had been in the moment. There were never any promises, any discussion of commitment. He had just assumed that things would continue, that Sarah would be part of his future.

Then he thought back to his conversation with Ben a few hours earlier. Ben had been such a key member of the department since Ray was first elected. More importantly, he had become a close friend and confidant. Ray considered what Ben's retirement would mean to him and to the department, and then his focus shifted to Sue, who more than once in recent months had mentioned wanting to take her life in a new direction, perhaps finding a man and starting a family, or possibly doing something different professionally, maybe both.

He pushed all these thoughts back. There was a murderer out there. He had an obligation to Brenda Manton to bring the killer to justice. That was his mission for the near future.

After cleaning up the kitchen, Ray settled at his computer and quickly checked his email. Then he Googled Rod Gunne. He clicked on the first pick and his screen filled with the home page of Rod Gunne's sophisticated Website. Ray turned his attention to the list of Webcasts of Gunne's sermons. He watched one, a tightly edited message less than 15 minutes in length, then a second. He pulled a legal pad from a desk drawer and starting making notes. First he analyzed the structure and organization of each short sermon. Then he noted the topic and message. Finally, he speculated on the intended audience. Several hours flew by as he worked his way through the whole menu of talks. Afterward, he opened his word processor and quickly keyed his observations into a document.

Wide awake, in spite of the hour, he moved to his writing desk—a sturdy, handcrafted piece of furniture that allowed him to stand while writing. He retrieved his favorite fountain pen and his journal and wrote a long summary of the Manton murder. He noted the lack of any strong suspects and speculated on the unlikely possibility of the crime being a random event, perpetrated by someone who had nothing more than an incidental relationship with Manton.

He mulled over the missing laptop. Might it be an important element in the case, or would a high-end computer be something a thug might grab at the end of a vicious assault? Ray's entry was mostly questions.

Then he reflected on his conversation with Sarah. This entry was short. He was still puzzling over what had happened, not comfortable yet with the possible conclusions. He closed the journal and returned it and the pen to their places under the top of the desk.

Before retiring, he thought again about what to do with his collection of journals. Their content was very personal; he was discomforted by the thought of anyone else reading them. Perhaps he should gather them up in a garbage bag and put them in the trash. He opened his closet and looked at the stack. He reached up and randomly pulled one from the middle and started to read.

The entry was about a phone call from his mother telling him that his father had had a stroke and was hospitalized. At that time Ray was teaching at a University three states away. The rest of the journal entry was about Ray's relationship with his father. In the extensive essay, he reflected on his sometimes-troubled relationship and how, over the years, he had come to understand and accept his father's alcoholism. He also talked about how their relationship had strengthened during the last years after his father had finally stopped drinking. He closed the journal and thought about what he had just read. He put it back on the shelf, realizing that he wasn't ready to part with his journals yet.

31

~~~~~~~~

"You're in rather late today," observed Sue.

Ray was working at his computer. He looked up at her and smiled.

"I seldom beat you to the office, and never by two or three hours," she continued. "Were you off on some special investigation, perhaps checking on the steelhead in a local stream while looking for Tristan Laird?"

"That's really good, Sue. I wish I had thought of that. More than once I've solved a crime walking a stream with a fly rod in my hand. Your brain gets a chance to work out there without all the buzz of an office.

"The truth is that I stayed up way too late. And I did something that I don't think I've ever done before, not since college, anyway. I overslept." Ray looked slightly abashed. "When I first awakened, it was light. Which I thought was rather peculiar, and when I looked at my watch it was after nine. My first thought was to go into panic mode, and then I decided to just take it easy, to kick back and go slow. I even took time to make a real breakfast."

"Well, you look rather pleased with yourself."

Ray took in her comment. He wasn't feeling jubilant, but he wasn't sad, either. Not like he had been last evening.

"You did the right thing," said Sue. "You've been looking very tired and tense. I've been worried about you."

Ray could tell from the tone of her voice that her concern was genuine. In recent years he had come to depend on Sue. She was smart and insightful, and she often intuited things that he missed. "Anything new?" he asked.

"I spent most of last evening and early this morning doing computer searches and looking through and adding to our investigative notes."

"It's good that one of us is on task."

"Yes," said Sue. "What would happen if we had real lives? What would it be like to go to a movie, or spend the night chatting with friends at a bar?"

"Tell you what. I've got tickets for the simulcast of the opera on Saturday. And after I'll take you to a restaurant where you can't even order a burger with fries. They don't have the ingredients on the premises. But the good news is that you can drink wine. I'll be the designated driver."

"Is your current love interest away this weekend?"

"It's a long story," replied Ray.

"Opera? I'm not sure. What's playing?"

"*Hamlet*. You'll love it. Very uplifting. Early on the ghost of the dead king appears and identifies the perps that offed him. Justice is wrought by the closing curtain. And in between lots of blood and gore."

"That's what we need, a ghost," said Sue. "You didn't happen to be talking to one last night?"

"I wish. The thing that kept me up," began Ray, "was that I got on Rod Gunne's Website and started listening to his sermons. I got hooked and went through the entire series."

"Are you a convert?" asked Sue, a wry smile forming on her face.

"Sort of," he responded. "He's good. He's staked out a target audience and created a message that would appeal to them. I'm impressed by how he uses words, images, and music to communicate with his followers. And as you observed when the two of us looked at his Website, Gunne, or the people he hires, really know how to use technology." Ray paused for a moment, then continued, "The thing that really knocked me over was his mission statement, or I guess I should say the mission statement for the church. It's a bit buried in the Website. Did you notice it?"

"I don't think so, nothing comes to mind," Sue responded. "What's the big deal?"

"It's labeled as the *mission statement*," said Ray, "but it's not one for the church, it's his personal mission statement. Gunne writes that through his close reading of scripture he has had personal conversations with God and he, Gunne, has been given the mission of correcting old thinking and making God's teaching relevant to a modern world. He goes on to say that he has been inspired to create an entirely new religious paradigm. And if you keep that in mind when you read the sermons, you can see how he's developing a very clear message."

"What did you learn from the sermons?" Sue asked.

Ray looked down at the notes he had made on a legal pad and glanced at a printed copy of the summary he keyed last night. "First, and this isn't about message, but it's important, is time. Gunne knows what every good eighth-grade teacher knows. If you want people to listen, talk at them for fifteen minutes or less and give them one or two things to remember. Every one of his messages is less than fifteen, usually around twelve minutes. Have you watched any of them?" he asked.

"Not really."

"Well, you should. They are skillfully produced. There's a story line, theme music, and the narrative develops his intended message."

"Which is?"

"Essentially, God wants you to be rich. You can enjoy the fruits of his kingdom while on earth if you just follow Reverend Rod's teaching, based rather loosely on scripture he cites and spins to fit his message. His theology is not completely original, but he's done a good job of making it all hold together fairly logically. And if you want to get the full pop of his teachings, he will personally pray for you for only pennies a day."

"Is that prey with an e? Anyone who sends money is the prey. Oh, come on Ray, the guy's a complete charlatan, a cyber Elmer Gantry."

"Sue, his message isn't all that bad. And it's mostly directed toward people who have been hurt economically the last few years. What he's telling people is that if they work hard, avoid debt, and stay away from gambling and drink or anything that wastes their resources needlessly, God will reward them. I suspect that message could be very helpful to many people."

"Give me a break."

"Look, Sue, if you drink, smoke, gamble, and have a messy personal life, and are reckless with your money and then suddenly you change your ways, you probably will have more money. It's a very positive philosophy."

"Okay," said Sue, "That's all well and good, but he's making a killing off something any fool should be able to figure out. And he's invoking some weird theology he's created to sell the product. I've never seen such a slick operation," Sue concluded emphatically.

"But as far as I can see, it's all very legal. And one of the great things about our country is that you get to believe or not believe in anything you want." Ray chuckled. "Gunne is living proof that if you follow his theology, you too can be rich. And he has figured out how to use technology to bring his message to a worldwide audience."

"I'm always amazed at how nonjudgmental you are, Ray."

"It makes the job a lot easier. I just focus on what's legal and what isn't legal. Worrying about who's a charlatan and who isn't requires too much psychic energy."

"So much for Gunne, did you follow up on Richard Kinver?" asked Ray.

"Yes. There is no record that he was ever involved in any arsons or suspicious fires, not even the one at his gravel pit."

"How about domestic runs?"

"Same. Like Ben told us, Kinver was apparently protected under Orville's friends and family policy," said Sue. "No police reports were ever filed. His marriages and divorces are part of public records, he's had three marriages, two divorces, and it looks like the third one is in process. His main residence is in foreclosure, and the property that the business sets on is also in the early stages of foreclosure."

"He probably inherited the business property free and clear," said Ray. "So he was obviously borrowing on that property to generate some money. But times are tough; I bet most of the contractors in the region are in great financial difficulty, so Kinver is hardly unique in that department. What do you do when your cash flow suddenly ends for a year or two or three?"

"I don't know, I can't imagine," said Sue. "It takes my whole income to cover my modest life style. But while we're talking about money, we've never really looked at Manton's finances. Perhaps we've been too fixated on looking for a personal relationship between Manton and her assailant."

"What do we know about her financial situation?" asked Ray.

"Not much. I checked the tax records; there are no liens against her property. From all appearances, she was relatively affluent compared to most of the artists I know in the area."

"True. Affluence is always relative, depending on where you are on the food chain. To a lot of the locals Manton would have looked quite well off. Could someone have been trying to borrow or extort money from her? For example, what if Kinver was trying to get money from her. Looks like he's pretty desperate right now. Manton refuses, and he goes crazy and offs her."

"That much rage?" asked Sue.

"Well, probably not. But you never know."

"And Kinver's alibi checked out. I talked with Mike McFarland. He said he and Richard were at a conference in Lansing. They came back early Thursday morning. I never went further than that. I've always found McFarland pretty reliable," said Sue.

"How about Manton's cell phone?" asked Ray, changing the direction of the conversation.

"Her carrier finally emailed me a copy. I could have gone to one of the snoop services and for a hundred bucks gotten the info in less than 24 hours. Doing it the right way takes over a week."

"And?"

"Just starting on that, Ray. I desperately need some time to start pulling together loose ends. We've been really scattered in this investigation. It will be wonderful if I get tomorrow to work on some of these things." Sue paused for a long moment. "Opera and dinner. Does this mean we would both take Saturday off?"

"Yes," said Ray.

"You're on, Ray. And I'm going to wear a dress and get my hair done. And I'll have the Saturday shift in place so neither of us is on call."

32

Early Saturday morning Ray was at a crime scene. He separated himself from the large group of emergency workers and walked back up the two-track and a long line of police and fire vehicles to meet Sue. "Your hair looks terrific," he said as the two approached one another.

"I always try to look my best when going to a murder. It's all part of reinforcing an image and building the brand," her tone was sarcastic. She paused for a moment and looked toward the scene at the end of the road. "I thought short of a nuclear attack or natural disaster, I had built a firewall sufficient to give us a day off. What's going on?"

"A 911 call just after first light. Some birders found the still smoldering remains of a pickup truck. The Township Fire Department was dispatched and Brett arrived shortly thereafter. After he ran the plates, he called me directly, and then I called you."

"I was just waking up when you called me. You said something about a body. Do you have an ID?"

"The truck belongs to Richard Kinver. There is a body, burned beyond recognition, in the cab of the truck."

They turned in the direction of the truck. It sat at the terminus of the road end, beyond was a sand dune, shelf ice, and the big lake.

"Are the people who called it in still here?" Sue asked.

"I talked to them as soon as I got here. Took a statement and got their names and addresses. They were pretty shaken by the experience. It was just two of them, husband and wife. Up for the weekend from Kalamazoo."

"Nothing like a weekend of birding in God's country," said Sue. "How about Dyskin?" asked Sue, referring to the medical examiner.

"He's come and gone. Took one look at the remains and said they should go to the forensic pathologist in Grand Rapids."

"How about the scene," asked Sue.

Ray didn't respond, he looked lost in thought.

"What's going on?" asked Sue, nudging him.

I was thinking about the Robert Frost poem, "Fire and Ice."

"I don't know it," said Sue.

Ray recited the short poem:

Some say the world will end in fire,
Some say in ice.
From what I've tasted of desire
I hold with those who favor fire.
But if it had to perish twice,
I think I know enough of hate
To say that for destruction ice
Is also great
*   And would suffice.*

"So assuming that it's Richard Kinver in the truck, what got him killed, desire, hate, or something else?" Ray's question wasn't directed at Sue. Then he turned his attention back to her. "What did you ask me?"

"The scene? What about the scene?"

"You won't be happy. Between the effects of the fire and people tromping around, the scene has been pretty much destroyed. They told me that the tires were still burning when they arrived and part of the interior was engaged, so everything has been sprayed with foam. They said that initially they didn't see the body."

"Well, let's get everyone back so I can get in and photograph the scene. Then we can get the body out of here and the truck hauled away before the gawkers finish with their morning coffee." Sue looked directly at Ray, "We need to get this done. I'm on my way to my first opera today, and I don't want to miss the opening curtain."

Several hours later Ray and Sue grabbed two of the remaining seats in the front row at the State Theatre in Traverse City. Sue turned around and scanned the audience. "We're the youngest people here," she said in a low tone just as the houselights began to dim.

At the end of the opera, after all the curtain calls, the house lights at both the Met and the State Theatre came up. Sue and Ray were at the end of the line in the slowly emptying theater.

Sue stopped and turned toward the now blank screen that had brilliantly reflected intense passion and anger for close to four hours. "That's what we need."

"What?"

"That's what we need," she repeated, "a ghost."

"I think we have one," responded Ray. "Tristan Laird."

33

~~~~~~~~

Sue's Jeep was parked twenty yards back from the blackened area where Richard Kinver's truck had been discovered little more than twenty-four hours before. Ray could see her beyond the scene, out on the shelf ice, with Simone off lead, scampering around near her. Ray walked out onto the ice, now extending forty or fifty yards from the shore, increasing in thickness toward the leading edge, where floating chunks of ice had been thrown onto the shelf during the last big storm.

Simone barked a greeting, dashed to Ray, tail wagging, begging to be picked up. Ray held her in his arms, scratching her head, and taking several sloppy kisses on the cheek.

"You have a way with women," joked Sue.

"Did I tell you how nice you looked in a dress yesterday," was Ray's opening gambit, noting Sue was in the department's winter uniform, her beautifully coiffed hair now covered by a thick, blue, stocking cap with the department emblem stitched on the front.

"I'm happy you noticed, and that you are able to mention it. You're always so professional, I'm not sure what you recognize and what you don't."

"There's nothing that says female officers can't wear skirts," Ray countered.

"And skirts would be terrific when you're trying to run a bad guy to ground in deep snow."

"How's Simone?"

"She's good and wonderful company, but she's spending more time with the dog sitter than me. Sometimes she ends up being boarded there several days in a row. Wonderful people, they keep her in the house, but I feel guilty. It's not a good situation, I'm trying to decide what to do."

Ray looked out at the big lake. There was no wind, the water's surface mirrored the sky in the early morning light. "There's a hint of spring," said Ray. "We're supposed to have clear weather and sun today and tomorrow."

"Good, I need the sun." Looking back at the shore, Sue asked, "Assuming it was Kinver's body in the truck, what do you think happened? He didn't strike me as a suicidal type."

"No," Ray agreed. "Never can dismiss any possibility, but suicide seems unlikely."

"We should have the results of the preliminary autopsy by tomorrow afternoon. If I can find and get Kinver's dental records faxed to the pathologist tomorrow morning, we can probably have a positive identification, also."

"I didn't look at the body too closely," admitted Ray. "When you were photographing, did you see any wounds?"

"Ray, if there were any wounds, they would not have been visible. It was bad." Sue let her comment hang for a long time. "I think that got to me, the condition of the body, maybe the smell of burnt rubber and flesh."

"So we have three arsons, two homicides—well, one homicide, one suspected homicide. And a murderer who likes fire," observed Ray.

"And how is Kinver part of this? Why did someone need him dead? Is there a killer out there who might think we know more than we do?" asked Sue.

"Several days ago we were talking about Kinver's alibi."

"Yes, Mike McFarland," said Sue.

"We need to bring County Commissioner McFarland in for a conversation. Now that Kinver is dead, I wonder if his memory of his time with Kinver in Lansing might have changed."

Sue pulled a notebook from her jacket pocket, flipped to the first blank page, and jotted McFarland's name.

"What do we tell the news media?" Sue asked.

"Tomorrow and maybe the next day we can get by with the victim has yet to be identified. Then we'll figure out what to do," answered Ray.

"What was he doing here in the middle of the night?"

"Perhaps he was killed somewhere else and brought here for cremation."

"That would have been considerate," said Sue. "Bring him to one of the loveliest beaches in the region and send him to the afterlife on a Chevrolet pyre." She paused briefly, and turned back toward the lake. "So what's going on with Sarah?"

"You're changing the subject," protested Ray.

"You looked like you were becoming a couple."

"I told you yesterday."

"You didn't tell me very much. Like most guys, you're quite laconic when it comes to anything that involves feeling." Sue looked thoughtful. "Well, that's not quite true, you're better than most guys, but you're still very guarded."

"Thanks, and I don't know what to tell you. Her job at Leiston went away. She had this terrific job offer in Chicago where she's going to make a lot of money. I'm here, she's there, and she says she loves being back in the city. That's all I know."

"Well, how do you feel?"

"I don't know. I enjoyed being with her. And I'm amazed at how quickly everything changed."

"And you're not going to resign your job and follow her to Chicago?"

"No, and I don't think she wants that either," said Ray, setting Simone down.

"Are we heading back to the office?" asked Sue.

"No, I think you and Simone deserve some quality time together."

"How about you?"

"I might bring a kayak over, cruise up and down the shelf ice for awhile."

"You and the young doctor?" she asked playfully.

" You know everything."

"Yep."

34

As Ray settled onto the small oak bench in the mudroom, he could hear the hubbub of friendly voices within and smell the rich aroma of skillfully prepared food. He pulled off his boots and put on a pair of soft moccasins that he had brought along. Sunday night dinner with his friends at Marc and Lisa's house had become a tradition. In recent weeks, however, the demands of his work had kept him away.

He pushed his way into the kitchen, greeted first by his friend Nora and her two dogs, Falstaff and Prince Hal. After a short flurry of welcoming barks and wags, the dogs wandered away and Ray was able to hand Lisa two bottles of wine for the meal.

"Sorry all I can do is bring wine this week," he said.

"What do you mean, just wine," retorted Marc. "You're providing the main course, that beautiful steelhead that you brought us a few weeks ago. I froze it so we could have it on a special occasion. I'm going to steam it in white wine."

"What else is on the menu?" asked Ray.

"Marc's been experimenting with bread again," said Lisa. "I don't think he's going to be happy until we build a brick oven. If we ever get around to redoing the kitchen that'll probably be part of it."

"No," said Marc. "If I'm going to go to all that trouble, I want something really big. It will have to be out in the yard."

"Maybe you're on the verge of starting a new business," joked Ray.

"If my investments don't get better, it's something I'll probably have to do," said Marc.

"Don't get him started, Ray. We now have a rule around here that Marc doesn't get to talk about the Wall Street robbers, at least not in my presence," said Lisa.

Ray chuckled, "My financial advisor said I shouldn't look at my monthly reports. He said I should try to focus on the big picture. I should probably only look at what's going on with my investments every five years."

"You're kidding," said Marc.

"No," said Ray. "And he told me this with a straight face. So I'm following his advice. Every month, when the statement arrives, I open the envelope and then shred the contents without looking at them. It's one less thing to get upset about."

"I saw you at the simulcast of the opera yesterday," said Nora. "You and that pretty young woman from your department." Nora, now in her late 80s, and Ray had been friends for years. When he was in high school and college, Ray had done odd jobs for Nora and her husband, Hugh. They were summer people then, living in Grosse Pointe, but spending much of July and August at their home on the Lake Michigan shore. Nora's roots ran deep in the area, and she had become an authority on local history. In addition to being a good friend, she had proven to be an important source when Ray needed background information about families and events that had occurred over the past decades.

"You sort of showed up at the last minute, just before the curtain, when the only seats were right up in front. Did you get a sore neck looking at the screen?" she asked.

"It wasn't too bad," said Ray.

"And where is Sarah?" asked Nora. "It wouldn't be like you, but is something going on between you and what's her name, Sue? I mean, you never know about men."

Before he could answer, Lisa was herding them to the dinner table and pouring wine for the appetizer course. She removed an extra place setting, an indication that she had anticipated that Sarah would accompany Ray.

"So what's going on with Sarah?" Nora asked again.

Ray explained briefly why Sarah was moving to Chicago.

"How do you feel about that?" asked Nora, falling into the patter of her former profession.

"No therapy tonight, Nora," said Lisa, with a smile. "Let's focus on Marc's wonderful cooking."

"I'm trying to do local," said Marc. "But that's hard in the dead of winter. Although with the help of a freezer and one jar of canned jam, I almost made it."

Ray examined the appetizers Lisa placed in front of each of them, small perfectly formed quiches. "Looks beautiful Marc. All local?"

"Pretty much. Morel mushrooms we picked and dried last spring, locally produced raclette cheese, local organic eggs, but I can't vouch for the butter, cream, or scallions."

"I want you to know what a special friend you are," said Lisa. "Marc used his last jar of thimbleberry jam to make the dessert. And speaking of our carbon footprint, what do you think of the environmental implications of our travel to the tip of the Keweenaw Peninsula to compete with the bears so we can make a few jars of jam?"

"Lisa, no one was talking about our carbon footprint," retorted Marc.

Ray helped Lisa clear away the appetizer plates as Marc plated the main course, pieces of poached steelhead with a delicate sauce and green beans, carefully steamed to ensure the best color and retain a bit of crispiness.

Lisa poured wine from a freshly opened bottle into clean glasses. Once they were settled at the table again, Ray asked Nora, "Do you know anything about a man called Tristan Laird?"

"Who?" asked Nora, after swallowing her first bite of fish.

"Tristan Laird," repeated Ray.

"Why should I know him?" she asked.

"He is a man who's probably in his late 30s. It has been reported that he often camps out in the National Shoreline or in the woods adjacent to the park."

"Maybe he's the son of Lorna of the dunes."

"Who? Isn't she a character in a Victorian novel?" asked Ray.

"No Ray, not Lorna Doone, Lorna of the dunes," said Nora, with obvious amusement. "It was a while back, maybe before your time. Late

50s, early 60s, but it was all the buzz one season. That's all the summer people talked about. It was a great story. Some young woman, supposedly a graduate of one of those girls' schools back east, when there were still girls' schools, had gone native. People would talk about seeing her on the beach, dressed in animal skins, her Phi Beta Kappa key glistening in the sunshine."

"Any truth to it?" asked Lisa.

"I don't think so," answered Nora. "Hugh and I spent so much time wandering the beaches and canoeing along the shore, if Lorna had been there we would've seen her. It was a good story, folks had a lot of fun talking about her, and by the next summer they'd forgotten her. I've got to say, it was a lot more fun than all of this chatter about the cougar that I've never seen."

"So you don't think you've ever seen Tristan Laird? He's supposed to do a lot of kayaking, even in the winter."

"I thought you were the only one nutty enough to kayak out beyond the shelf ice. No, Ray, I don't think I can help you with that one. Lots of strange people wander past my place all year long. But I don't know any Tristan Laird."

"Have you noticed anything strange tonight?" said Marc, directing his question to Ray.

"What do you mean?" asked Ray.

"I told Lisa that I would take her to Key West for a week if she could get through an entire meal without asking you about your latest investigation," said Marc.

"We're not even at dessert yet," said Lisa. "Why did you bring it up?"

"It's wonderful spending several hours not talking about it," said Ray. "Tell me about this thimbleberry tart," he said, moving the conversation away from the investigation.

35

Way before first light the next morning, Monday, Ray was wide-awake. The relaxed feelings he had experienced the previous evening were gone. He was tense, he needed some answers, and he needed to get the investigation moving forward.

He was able to spend several hours at the office very productively before the business of the day got started. He was always amazed by the amount of paperwork required, even in a very small police agency.

A few minutes after 9 a.m., Sue arrived, County Commissioner Mike McFarland in tow.

"What's going on, Sheriff," McFarland demanded. "Your deputy here had me on the phone just after seven. In the winter I try to sleep in. What's so important?"

"Have a seat," directed Ray. "I need to talk to you about Richard Kinver."

"What's the problem?" Mike McFarland asked, his tone hostile. He took off his heavy brown canvas jacket, dropped it on the back of a chair, and settled across from Ray at the conference table. He was wearing a green flannel shirt and red suspenders.

"Last week you told Sue that you and Kinver were in Lansing together. Isn't that what you told her?" said Ray motioning toward Sue.

"Yeah, that's what I told her. Something wrong with that."

"So you're telling me that you were with Kinver all evening that night?"

"Well, more or less. The meeting ran late, then we went back to the motel."

"Were you two sharing a room?"

"No," answered McFarland.

"Did you see Kinver the next morning?" asked Ray.

"No, Richard is an early riser. I like to sleep in. He was probably on the road before I got up."

"But you told my deputy, that you were with Richard. You didn't say anything about not seeing him the next morning. In fact, as I understand it, you gave her the distinct impression that you were with Richard on Wednesday and Thursday."

"I was with him all day Wednesday, and he was staying Wednesday night. What's the diff?"

"Here is the diff," said Ray. "We found a burned-out Chevy pickup truck early Saturday morning. There was a body inside, burned beyond recognition. When we ran the plates the vehicle belonged to Richard Kinver. We won't have a positive identification on the body until later today, but assuming that it's the body of Richard Kinver, where he has been recently and what he was doing has become very important. His name has come up several times in the case of the assault and murder of Brenda Manton. Kinver used you as an alibi, and we accepted your word."

Ray and Sue sat in icy silence, letting the news of Kinver's death soak in. Finally McFarland spoke, "It was no big deal."

"What's no big deal?" asked Ray.

"Well, before we parted for the night, Richard said, 'If anyone ever asks, I was here all night.' And then he went on and said something to the effect that you never know when you have to make a run."

"What's all that about?" asked Ray.

"It was sort of a code," said McFarland. "I've been hanging out with Richard since we were in second grade together. By the time we're in high school, he always had a steady girlfriend and a couple of other girls on the side. When he was heading off to spend time with someone other than his main girlfriend, he'd always say, 'I got to make a run.' That was the code. He didn't change over the years, he had wives and he had girlfriends. He often used me for cover. He'd tell me he was making a run just in case his wife called."

"So you lied to the wife?" asked Sue.

"No, I just knew not to answer the phone."

"So who are these women?" asked Ray.

"Well, I assumed the run Wednesday night had to do with someone in Grand Rapids. But there were lots of gals. He was always doing favors for women. Plowing drives, dropping off a pickup load of firewood. It was sort of a trade-off." McFarland paused for a minute, "It wasn't just local women, he also had something going with some of the cottagers. Some women are up here all summer, mostly alone. He'd strike up an acquaintance when he was delivering topsoil or bark or laying down new gravel on a drive. He just had this knack for knowing who might be interested." McFarland paused again and looked thoughtful for a long moment. "I guess today you'd say he had some kind of sex addiction, that he needs some kind of therapy. But, hell, it was really no big thing. No one was getting hurt. Just people being people. Nothing wrong with that."

"You said that you and Richard have been friends since elementary school. What's been going on in his life recently? Is it possible that he was suicidal? Do you have any reason to believe that someone might have wanted him dead?" asked Sue.

"Like most of us, things have been rough for Richard the last couple of years. There ain't been hardly no work, he's had to give up or sell off his best equipment, what he's got left is mostly junk. And I know he's been borrowing money on the yard and gravel pit. He's pretty much got his back against the wall. Thank God he had his county commissioner's salary and the health insurance.

"But going back to your question. There is no way that Richard would ever kill himself. Not a chance. He would figure out some way to keep going. Sheriff, that body found in the truck, if it's Richard's body, he was murdered. You can take that to the bank."

"What's going on with his marriage? I heard he was getting a divorce."

"That's old news, Ray. His wife left town with someone she met at Art's Tavern. Suppose to have a house on Big Glen and another one in Arizona, Florida, someplace. I hear the guy's old enough to be her grandfather."

"Is the divorce through?" asked Sue.

"I don't know that. He never said. I never could see why he bothered to get married, anyhow. And Cindy, that's the one we're talking about, was a big part of his current money problems. He did everything he could to keep her happy, and when the money was gone, she was, too."

"Mike, did Richard say or do anything that might suggest that he was in trouble or afraid?" asked Ray.

"No. He was just the same old Richard. If there was something really wrong, he didn't share with me."

"Brenda Manton," said Sue, "Did he ever mention her to you?"

"That's the woman that got killed a couple weeks back?"

"Yes," said Sue.

"He did a lot of work for her last year or the year before. Excuse my French ma'am, but he was always telling me about the great tits she had. He also joked about her, he thought all this green building stuff was a bunch of malarkey."

"Do you think that anything happened between them?" asked Ray.

"No, I don't think so. He hasn't talked about her in months."

"I saw one of Richard's end loaders at the new church off of 22. Had Richard gotten religion or was that just a job?" asked Ray.

"Like I was saying, I've known Richard for decades. And I've never seen him involved in religion, let alone going to church. But it's true, he started going there sometime last spring. Go figure. And he wanted me to come with him for services. Several times he tried to talk me into it. I think we parted ways on that one."

"What was the attraction for him?" asked Sue.

"It was kind of crazy that. He was telling me that God or Jesus, I could never figure out which, wanted him to be rich, and if he could just settle down and get some focus things would turn around in his life. Now I was brought up Catholic, and I can't say I'm religious, but I know that isn't right," said McFarland.

"Do you know if Richard developed a friendship with the minister up there, Rod Gunne?" asked Sue.

"Can't say for sure, but I wouldn't be surprised," said McFarland. "All I can tell you is that I haven't seen him around much this winter.

Usually we do a lot of ice fishing and hanging out, but not this year. In the past when Richard was real scarce, it was 'cause there was a new woman. I just thought that was the case."

"Mike, can you think of anyone who would want to murder Richard?" asked Ray.

"Richard, he was a friend of everyone. I don't know what else to tell you, Ray."

"How about husbands and boyfriends of some of the women Richard was seeing?" asked Sue.

"Well, there's that, isn't there? I think Richard was pretty smart about that. For his girlfriends he seemed to pick women that didn't want any entanglements either. He always referred to that as his 'sport fucking.' It was just an event, nothing more."

"Do you know where Richard was living? We heard he had lost his house," said Sue.

"Well, last I heard he was staying in an old house trailer they have up at the yard. Must have been quite a comedown from the place on the lake. That was something. I could never figure out how he swung that."

"We're going to need your help, Mike. First, we need you not to say anything about this conversation or the fact that Richard is dead. We have to confirm his identity and notify next of kin. We will probably have that done by late afternoon. Then, we need you to think about anything that might be useful in our investigation. Make some notes, give us a call, stop by and talk."

"I'll do that, Ray. I'll do that. I can't believe he's dead. It doesn't seem possible."

"Before you go," said Sue, "What can you tell me about his family?"

McFarland didn't answer immediately. He pulled at his ear and then looked back at Sue, "Not much, the old folks have been gone a long time, his parents passed in recent years. He was an only child. He used to talk about cousins downstate somewhere, that's all I know."

36

When Sue returned to Ray's office after walking Mike McFarland out to his car, Ray was busy at his keyboard, converting his penciled notes from several sheets of a legal pad to a word-processing file.

"That was interesting," said Sue.

"Yes," agreed Ray. "But what did we learn? Give me 10 or 15 minutes to type this up and then we can go through it and see if we heard the same things and if there's anything we can use."

"Okay. Can I get you some fresh coffee?"

Ray made a face. "How about just filling my water bottle?"

"Sure," Sue responded, plucking his aluminum bottle off the desk before heading out. A few minutes later she returned. "There's been a break-in at the West Shore Village Medical Clinic. Jake is at the scene. The staff arrived this morning to find the place torn apart. Jake says it appears that access was gained by cutting through the roof. He's trying to keep people away so I can have access to the scene before it's completely disrupted. He's having trouble with a doc. The guy has patients waiting and Jake describes his behavior as belligerent and uncooperative. I think I should get over there asap."

"We'll talk on the way," said Ray. "I want to meet this physician."

"How so?" asked Sue.

"I'll explain on the way."

Ray settled into the passenger seat as Sue sped toward the scene.

"You're getting quite comfortable being chauffeured about," Sue observed.

"Yes," agreed Ray. "I don't know why I insisted on being the driver all my adult life. It's really nice to sit and look around and have time to think without concentrating on the road."

"You were going to tell me about the physician that's giving Jake a hard time?"

"Yes, and I don't even know if it's the same person, but Hannah Jeffers, the cardiologist, told me one of the reasons she came to this area was at the urging of an old love interest from college or medical school."

"Are you seeing her?" Sue asked. "Hannah Jeffers."

"Let me finish what I was telling you." Ray grumped. "Hannah said over the years they had both changed a lot and the relationship came to an end after they had dinner one evening with Rod Gunne. She said her friend, I think she said his name was Bob, was very taken with Gunne and his theology of wealth. Now here's my point, Sue, two weeks ago I had never heard of Rod Gunne. Since then he just keeps popping up."

"Funny how that happens, isn't it? And Jeffers, going back to my question?"

"God, are you nosey. And, no, I'm not seeing her, not in the romantic way if that's what you're asking. She was looking for someone to go kayaking with, and Saul Feldman told her to look me up. She did.

Enough of this, I was really ready for a conversation about Richard Kinver," said Ray. "As soon as we get done with this, I want to focus on Kinver."

Sue turned off the highway and, slowing, rolled down the main street of the village, four blocks long, the final two blocks before the "T" intersection at the end of the village showing the last vestiges of what had once been the commercial district of a small lumbering town. The only year-round businesses left were a grocery store, a tavern, and the post office. Several seasonal businesses, an ice cream and fudge shop, and a too-artsy souvenir store sat empty in the cold morning light.

The West Shore Village Medical Clinic stood at the base of the intersection, in a building that had seen many uses over the years as a hardware store, a dry goods store, and a marine supply. In its current iteration the structure had been stripped back to its block walls and converted to an attractive, well-equipped clinic.

The large patient parking lot at the site of the clinic was partially filled with cars. Jake Jacobson's sheriff's car was parked at an oblique angle near the main door of the clinic. He was standing on the outside with several people who appeared to be part of the clinic's staff. Sue parked her Jeep behind Jake's cruiser.

As they approached, Jake seemed relieved to see them. He did the introductions. Dr. Bob Adamo seemed to be in charge. He glared at Ray in obvious agitation, his face and mostly-bald head flushed with anger. Adamo looked thin and athletic. Ray thought he was probably a long-distance runner.

"Look, Sheriff," Adamo began, "I got sick people out here sitting in cars waiting to be seen. And the officer here won't even let us in to get started on the cleanup."

"Doctor, we will need some time. I suggest you and the staff explain to your patients that the clinic is not going to be open this morning." He could hear Adamo continue to talk at him as he turned and entered the building.

Ray, Sue, and Jake stood in the waiting room, Jake providing a quick account of what had happened since he had arrived. "The staff parks in a lot in the rear. The first person to arrive this morning, the receptionist, found the back door unlocked. Initially, she assumed one of the docs had come in early. She walked through, hung up her coat and went to start the coffee. That's when she noticed that the room where they keep meds had been ransacked. I guess Adamo arrived soon after, and she showed him what had happened, and he called it in. In the meantime he had her open the front door and allow people into the waiting room. He was most unhappy with me when I told him that his staff and patients had to vacate the building. After they were out, I did a quick walk through to make sure that the perp was no longer on the premises. That's when I discovered the hole in the roof in a back storeroom."

"Did Adamo or anyone assess what's missing?" asked Sue.

"There was a second doc here when I arrived. She said only the med room was hit, and she told me that they never have any narcotics here. She pointed out that they have signs on both doors stating just that."

"Guess they better put some signs on the roof too," quipped Sue.

"Let's seal off the building and give Sue time to work," said Ray. "I'll explain to the good doctor what we're doing and give him some time estimates."

37

"What did you find?" asked Ray, as Sue piloted the Jeep away from the village.

"Not much," she responded. "I've got some pretty good prints that are probably from the perp, and I've got some good photos of some footprints from the roof and interior. Looks like the guy was wearing tennis shoes."

"How much damage on the roof?"

"Not much," said Sue. "The perp knew what he was doing. He popped a vent cover, cut open some ductwork, came down through the suspended ceiling. I think we're looking for someone driving a pickup truck with a ladder rack, someone in the building trades who knows the layout of this building." Sue waited at the stop sign for several cars to pass, then turned left. "Did you talk to the doc, what's his name, Adams?"

"Adamo, Robert Adamo. And yes, after things were sort of squared away, we walked over to the tavern and had some coffee."

"So what's the deal with their security system? It didn't look like it had been activated."

"That's one of the first things I asked him."

"And?" Sue finally asked, impatiently.

"Adamo said that it was a continuous hassle. People were forgetting to set it or disarm it, and since they had never had a break-in, it was easier not to use it."

Sue paused, briefly, "What else did you learn from Adamo?"

"He's one unhappy, frustrated guy."

"How so?"

"He's upset about a whole litany of things. I should get combat pay, or at least the hourly rate of a good shrink for having to listen to him."

"Give me the gist."

"First, he can't stand winter any longer…"

"None of the rest of us can either," interrupted Sue. "Give me something original."

"Well, he thought he would like family practice, and he doesn't. Says his patients aren't very interesting. He said some stupid idealism kept him from pursuing a more remunerative specialty. And then he doesn't like his partner."

"I saw the name on the shingle, Shelley something, started with an M. What's wrong with Shelley?"

"Adamo says that she has a habit of not charging patients if they don't have any money. He says word is getting around and all the uninsured deadbeats in the county are filling their waiting room."

"Her only flaw?" asked Sue.

"One of many, actually. He's installed software that provides data that would help them increase the profitability of the practice. And apparently Shelley doesn't cooperate. Alas, I don't think this relationship can be saved."

"Anything else?" asked Sue, her eyes fixed on the road.

"Well, finally there was a rant against society in general. Something to the effect that only the best and brightest go to medical school, and if society doesn't pay them what they deserve, the best and brightest will do something else, and medicine will become a third-rate profession."

"That's pretty heavy," said Sue. "Did he mention anything about getting religion? Maybe something about getting God on the side of the best and brightest and being compensated accordingly."

"Well, not exactly," answered Ray, "He launched into this diatribe about how many of the illnesses they were treating were self-inflicted, and then he made the leap to The Church for the Next Millennium and how religion, or shall I say, this religion would help people improve their lives. Then he switched to a serious proselytizing mode, which gave me an opportunity to ask about the church, Rod Gunne, and Adamo's relationship with Gunne."

"You are so good. I can just see you in action, sitting there quietly, occasionally asking a question. So what did you learn?" probed Sue.

"Rod Gunne is a patient, and he got Adamo to come to church, and it's the first time he's ever found a faith that he could relate to. I told him we had visited the church, and we were very impressed. I talked about the wonderful artwork and then segued to the tragic death of Brenda Manton."

"Anything?"

"Not that I could put my finger on. But there was a definite change in the tone of the conversation. He made some clichéd response to what a tragedy her death was and then did his best to change the subject. After that point, he only wanted to talk about when we would find and apprehend the person who caused them to lose a half day's work. What do you think?" Ray asked.

"I think I should have joined you. They have great burgers at that tavern, and they make these killer sweet potato fries. And you'd like their surf and turf."

"What?"

"Just your style, Ray, a big helping of fried smelt, a half-pound burger, and fries on the side."

Ray exhaled loudly. "Maybe some of Adamo's depression is justified," he said.

38

～～～

"Where are you?" asked Sue as she read a preliminary copy of Richard Kinver's autopsy report.

"Down at the bottom," said Ray, "*Cause of Death and Manner of Death.*"

"So it was a bullet wound," said Sue. "With all the damage from the fire that wasn't apparent."

"And Richard Kinver was dead before he was torched—that eliminates the possibility of suicide. And he could've easily been killed somewhere else, driven to that road end, and then the truck was torched."

"I wonder why?" asked Sue.

"Another mystery," said Ray. "Maybe the perp wanted to get the truck to a place where it could be torched with little or no chance of being discovered before the fire had done its work."

"Well, it looks like the same perp. Using fire to erase evidence seems to be his MO," observed Sue.

"Now we have to work on motive. Let's hope we can come up with better possibilities than we were able to with Brenda Manton."

"Lots of possibilities," said Sue. "The husbands or lovers of his various women, things connected with his shaky finances." Sue paused and looked up at Ray, her face suddenly lighting with mirth. "Try this out. Kinver stops by to see one of his ladies and after he gets his jollies, he drops off a load of wet, green firewood."

Ray shook his head. "Well, wouldn't you be ticked if you got a bad load of firewood? Probably not a good exchange."

He moved to the whiteboard and began making a list. He looked over at Sue and said, "These are the things that we have to attend to immediately. Maybe you can get Brett Carty to help with the legwork. Mike McFarland told us he didn't know of any relative living in the area. I'd like to verify that before we do a press release and news conference. If there are cousins downstate, let's see if we can find them and let them know."

"This will be big news, Kinver was well-known in the county. And we should probably get this out before the evening news cycle." Ray listed *notification* and *news conference* on the board. Then he added, *cell phone records*. "Chances are that someone lured him out in the middle of the night. His cell phone records might tell us who did the calling."

"You know, Ray, if Kinver was wandering around in the middle of the night it would probably be for some woman."

"That just crossed my mind," he responded.

"In this case and the Manton murder we've always assumed that the perp was a man," said Sue. "What if?"

"The Manton assault just looks like something a man would do. Think about the violence and force."

"Yes, and somehow these two murders appear connected and maybe they are, but with two different murderers? How about Kinver killing Manton and then a woman killing Kinver?' Sue asked.

"Interesting possibility. Then there's the issue of Kinver's big Oshkosh plow. We sort of accepted the story that it was stolen."

"Yes," agreed Sue. "It just made no sense for him to be driving it. It was a vehicle easily identified as belonging to him, and why wouldn't he just use his own pickup for transportation? Plus, he had this alibi. We've never pursued the truck issue."

"So why would anyone have used the Oshkosh?" Ray probed.

After a long pause, Sue answered, "Other than the possibility of trying to put Richard Kinver at the scene of the assault, I can't think of anything else. And it did prove pretty useful in taking care of a couple of nosey police officers."

"Almost more than just taking care of," Ray added.

"The use of the truck is just bizarre. It makes no rational sense. Let's say Richard had nothing else to drive, he might use the Oshkosh, but we know that's not the case."

"And both the Oshkosh and the truck were burned in isolated spots, at road ends, in the middle of the night so any evidence that they might contain would be destroyed. And then the perp disappears. There are trails running off into the woods. So what if the person who dumped the vehicle walked back up a trail. And when they get back to the road they're in a remote location. So how did they get out of there, jog?"

"So you think maybe two people?" asked Sue. "Makes sense," she said, not waiting for him to answer. "And then we shift back to motive. We still don't know that much about Manton and why someone wanted her dead. But that someone had to know her well enough to know about Tristan Laird. And the night of the assault on Brenda they either saw Tristan or knew that there was a great possibility that he was in the area."

"But how did they know where to find him? Only..."

"We led the way," said Sue. "We made a path for them. All they had to do was follow our tracks."

"Who would tail us?" Ray asked.

"Maybe we weren't being tailed at all. Maybe they just saw us parked in the road, getting ready to hike to the tree house. They just put two and two together."

"But to put two and two together, you'd have to know about the elusive Tristan Laird. And what we know is that Brenda Manton and Molly Birchard are Tristan's keepers. So to know anything about Tristan, you have to know Molly and Brenda well. We are going to have to nail the reluctant-to-talk Molly down. We've been too damn gentle with her. Get her on the phone and get her in here."

Sue headed for the door, "I'll get Brett started, set up the briefing, and call Molly Birchard."

Ray returned to the autopsy. This time he read it from top to bottom. He had this sense that he was on the edge of putting it all together, that perhaps the key was somewhere in the report. All he had to do was connect the dots.

Ray was peering off into space, lost in thought when Sue suddenly reappeared. "Sorry to interrupt you, but Stephanie Janzen—the woman who thinks her parents have gone missing—is here. I've just had a word with her, and I think you should talk to her."

Ray could tell by Sue's tone that Janzen had information he needed to hear.

"Bring her in," he said.

A moment later Sue reappeared with Stephanie Janzen. After they had settled at the conference table, Sue said, "Please share with the sheriff what you just told me."

"Before I do that, there's something I want to tell you, Sheriff. After I left here the other day I went to the State Police. I think I did the same thing there that I did here. I told them about my father and demanded that they do something. A very patient desk sergeant explained to me, much as you had done, the parameters for labeling someone a missing person. So, I want to clear the air. I was probably aggressive and obnoxious, and I apologize.

"But I have to tell you that I just knew that something was wrong. I've stayed around town for a few days trying to be on vacation, but I couldn't stop thinking about this. So yesterday I went back out to the house, not actually to the house, but nearby. My father's got a big storage barn a couple of miles from his home on some vacant farmland. He keeps all his toys there. He's got a couple of sports cars, some antique tractors, and his big RV, the Bluebird. It was clear that no one had been in there, deep snow and no tracks. I brought some boots, but they weren't adequate for the job. Anyway, I hiked in and looked around, peeked in windows and the Bluebird is there, in the storage building. I could see it clearly through the window."

Ray looked across the table at Janzen, her large liquid eyes staring into his.

"Sheriff, I think I understand about missing persons, now. And I'm starting to comprehend how to approach things. I know you can't go knock down doors and start questioning people because some alienated child returns home for a few days after many years and wants to know why the world has changed. That said, something is wrong. I don't know if there is anything you can do about it, but something is very wrong."

Ray allowed her last sentence to hang while he thought about his response. He noted for the first time how attractive she was, her short hair enhancing her delicate features.

"Ms. Janzen, I can't tell you specifically what we will do. Detective Lawrence and I will have to discuss that. But I can tell you that we will start making some inquiries in the next few days and see where that leads us. There is no evidence of any criminal behavior, but I'll see what we can find. I can't tell you that we can necessarily solve this puzzle, but within the limits of the law we will do what we can."

"Thank you, Sheriff. Do you think I should hire a private investigator?"

"That's an option you might want to consider at some time. For now, why don't you give us a few days? How long are you going to be in the area?"

"By next weekend I should be on my way back."

"How about this," said Ray. "Let's meet on Friday afternoon and have a talk. Please give Sue the exact location of the storage building. And one more thing, would you stay away from your parents' home and avoid any contact with Rod Gunne? This is a very sensitive case, and I like to keep things rather low key. Can you do that?"

"Yes, I can."

"Friday," said Ray, "about 2:00 in the afternoon."

"I'll be here," Janzen said. "I can find my way out. Thank you for talking to me."

After she was gone, Sue asked, "What are you going to know on Friday that you don't know today?"

"Maybe nothing, but I wanted to get her promise that she wouldn't be lurking about. We have enough complications."

"What else?" asked Sue. "I can see something is really bouncing around that head of yours. Do I sense one of your cognitive leaps is bubbling to the surface?"

"I have this feeling that we're almost there. We're just not putting the pieces together." Ray stopped and changed direction. "One more thing for your list, Sue. Just to be on the safe side, request a report on Kinver's trailer. I'm going to run out for a bit and see if I can find Dell. He's probably as much next to kin as anyone Kinver has."

"Make sure you're back in time for the press conference," cautioned Sue.

"I will be. Promise."

39

Ray was rolling fast as he headed south on 22 toward Richard Kinver's excavation business. He was thinking about two things, how to break the news of Kinver's death to Dell and how much information to disclose at the news conference.

He had meant to check Dell's house first before driving up to the gravel pit, but he had been so lost in thought that he only remembered it just as he was turning into the business. Ray circled the front of the main building and not seeing Dell's truck, made a sweeping circle and headed back in the direction he'd come.

A few minutes later he pulled into Dell's carefully cleared drive. He didn't see Dell's pickup truck, a vintage fire-engine red Chevrolet. He suspected that it was behind the closed garage doors at the rear of the house.

He walked to the front door. He could hear the television blaring from the interior. He knocked loudly, no answer. He knocked a second time, and when there was no response he pushed the door open and yelled, "Dell, are you here?"

Dell poked his head around the corner into the living room. "Oh, Ray, I thought I heard something. Come on in. And close the door. I'm not heating the outside."

Ray walked through the dark interior of the living room toward the back of the house. Dell was in the kitchen. The volume on the television was still turned way up. Dell was struggling with the remote to get the sound turned down.

"Sorry about that, Ray. When I'm home alone I don't bother to put my hearing aids in. So I've got to crank up the TV most of the way if I want to hear. Want some coffee?" Dell asked, as he fished his hearing aids out of his shirt pocket, and then put them in his ears.

"Not for me, thanks," said Ray. "I've got something to tell you, and I need your help with a couple of things."

"Something wrong?" asked Dell.

"It's about Richard," said Ray. "It appears that he's been murdered."

Dell's body went limp, and he sagged into his chair. He said nothing.

"I am going to have a news conference later this afternoon. I wanted you to know before it was on television."

"When did it happen?" asked Dell.

"Saturday morning. It took us a couple of days to get a positive identification."

"I'm not following," said Dell.

"Dell, Richard's body, it had been burned beyond recognition. We had to rely on dental charts for positive identification."

Dell pulled himself from his chair. He went over to the wood stove, opened the door, stirred the coals around, and carefully laid in a couple of chunks of split oak. He walked back to the table and sat down across from Ray. "Don't know what to say. Richard, he wasn't the best person in the world, not the worst, either. But murder and fire. I don't see how he ever deserved that."

"I don't understand either," said Ray. "You feel up to answering a couple questions?"

"Sure. Go ahead."

"You know where Richard's been living lately?"

"Well, sometime in the late summer or fall he moved into the trailer up at the yard. That's after he lost the house to the bank. But then by winter he didn't seem to be using it anymore. I asked him about it, and he just sort of laughed. You know, he always treated me like a dumb old man. Like I didn't know what was going on, like my eyes and brain weren't working anymore. I mean, I don't hear too well, but I think everything else is still there. And what Richard didn't seem to understand was I've seen a hell of a lot of life."

"So, Dell, if he wasn't living in the trailer, have any idea where he might have been staying?"

"Ray, Richard prided himself on being the cock of the walk. There were always women coming around looking for him. I imagine he was just bedding down with one of them, maybe more."

"Dell, did you tell me that Richard couldn't drive the Oshkosh?"

"Richard could drive it," said Dell, "that is, after a fashion he could drive it. I mean he could get it in gear and go backwards and forwards, but he could never plow with it. The hydraulics, they were pretty shot, and he could never get the hang of the belly blade. He tried using it once around the shop in the winter, that heavy snow the first week of November. He just made a mess."

"Anyone else know how to drive the Oshkosh?"

" It's just the two of us, Ray. Everyone else's been laid off since August."

"Did Richard ever show anyone else the Oshkosh or let anyone else drive it?"

"I don't think so, not when I was around."

"Dell, you are known as one of the best diesel mechanics around. Did you ever work on a Bluebird?"

"What are you talking about Ray, a bus? I worked on a couple that the school district owned. That was way back, maybe 30 years ago, maybe more."

"No," said Ray. "I'm talking about a large RV, something you might have done in the last year or two."

"I think I know what you're talking about. Richard dragged me over to look at this big RV. It was in a huge storage barn. The owner couldn't get it started. I'm not sure it had been run in several years. It was an old Travelodge. And you're right, that was made by the Bluebird."

"What happened?" asked Ray.

"It needed a lot of work. I told them I'd have to have parts and diagrams and some manuals. I called down to the company, and they weren't much help. That part of the business has been closed down. So the old guy that owns it, he didn't want to mess with it. He bought something new."

"So what do you think, the man drove away for the winter?"

"Well that's the interesting part. He seemed to be in bad health. So Richard drove the man and his wife somewhere, I think he said Arizona. Richard told me he got paid plenty for doing the driving and an airplane ticket back. He said the guy even put him up in a hotel in Vegas as thanks. And Richard said he was also being well paid to look after the man's house during the winter."

"The man you're talking about, did you get his name?" asked Ray.

"No, I don't think we were ever introduced. I only saw him once."

"Do you know if Richard had any relatives in the area?"

"No," said Dell. "The old folks are long gone, his dad died about 15 years ago and his mom in the last couple. I'm not sure about the rest of the family. But at the funeral I bet you'll see a whole line of grieving women." Then he chuckled.

40

Ray made it back to the office just in time for the press briefing. Sue was already in the conference room chatting with the reporters when he arrived. There were only three reporters, two print—one from the regional daily and one from the county monthly—and one television reporter, with her cameraman.

Sue had produced a carefully written press release. Ray read that release and then answered questions, turning many of them over to Sue.

As soon as the briefing was over, Sue indicated with some urgency that they needed to talk.

"What's going on?" asked Ray.

"Molly Birchard has gone missing."

"What?" said Ray.

"I called her cell phone, and there was no answer, so I left a message. Then I walked over to dispatch to see if they have any other contact information for her, like her mother's phone number. Molly was on the day shift this weekend, but she didn't show up for work yesterday. She didn't call in, and they haven't been able to reach her. I called her mother, who was less than forthcoming in providing any information about the whereabouts of her daughter. I asked her if I could come visit her about five, and she agreed. I want you to come with me."

"So she worked Saturday," said Ray. "She would've known about Richard Kinver, or at least about his truck with the strong suspicion that it was Kinver's body that we found inside."

"That was my thought," said Sue. "Am I chauffeuring you again?"

"Absolutely. I'm really getting into having a driver," said Ray.

Ruth Birchard's house was on the south edge of the village in an area of the township beyond the village limits. It was one of a scattering of homes—mostly modulars, doublewides, and trailers—along a narrow twisting country road. Sue pulled into a small drive behind a large rusting Oldsmobile. The house, one story, with faded yellow siding, sagged into the side of a hill. Plastic geraniums, bleached to a whitish-pink, poked through a snow-covered flowerbox under a picture window.

Ruth Birchard pushed open a wooden storm door and held it for Sue and Ray as they entered the small, cluttered living room. "You want to come into the kitchen?" she asked. "We can sit at the table there and talk." She didn't wait for an answer; she just led them to the adjoining room. There was already a coffee pot and two cups with saucers on the table. She brought a third to the table as they settled. She poured coffee without asking them whether they wanted any.

Ray looked across the table at Ruth. Although he did not believe he had ever met her, she looked vaguely familiar. He noted that there was a striking similarity between Ruth and her daughter, Molly. Her face was deeply lined, her brown-gray hair, dull. Ray sensed anxiety and despair.

"We need your help," said Sue. "We need to know what's happened to Molly, where she is."

Birchard was slow in responding. It appeared that she was thinking about what she was going to say. "Is she in some kind of trouble?" she finally asked.

"She's not in trouble with us," responded Sue. "But she may be in some kind of trouble. As you know, her best friend was murdered. The sheriff and I have never believed that she's been totally truthful with us about what she might know about Brenda Manton's death. Now there is a second murder, it might be related to the first..."

"Second murder?" Ruth asked, the tension rising in her voice.

"Yes," said Sue. "Richard Kinver. It happened this weekend. It will be on the news tonight."

A long silence followed. Finally, Birchard responded, "Oh my God."

"Do you know Richard Kinver?" asked Sue.

"I've known him for a long time," she answered, her voice weary. "He started messing with Molly when she was in junior high. That's when she started hanging out with the wrong kids; he was at the center of the group. He was older, maybe a junior or senior. I knew he was trouble from the instant I saw him. I've always blamed Richard for getting her started with drugs, sex too.

"I don't think that she would have made it through high school if she hadn't gotten that scholarship to Leiston School. They had a special program back then to bring some local kids to the school. Molly was so good in art and writing, and not that bad of a student, either. Having a chance to go to Leiston really changed her life. She got to know some nice kids from all over the world, and it got her away from Richard, at least during the school year. But as soon as she was home for the summer, he was always hanging around." She sagged in her chair and looked defeated.

"After Leiston she got a scholarship to college, and things were going good for her. But then she had a bad marriage and moved back here, so I could help her look after her son. She's a really good potter, but how do you make a living doing that?" She paused for a long moment. "This job with the county was a good thing for her, a real lifeline."

"Has Molly been involved with Kinver recently?" asked Sue.

"He's always been around," Birchard answered. "He just can't leave her alone. He ruined her life. She can never say no to Richard. Never."

"So what is going on with Molly now?" asked Ray. "She didn't show up for work yesterday, and she didn't call in."

"She's in some kind of big trouble," Birchard answered, her voice barely audible.

"What kind of trouble?" pressed Ray.

"I don't know, Sheriff. She comes over here on Sunday and asks if I can look after my grandson, Scott, for a while. I'm thinking that she's talking about a few hours, but I come to understand very quickly she's talking about weeks. She tells me something bad is going on. She's got to get out of town. Go somewhere far away. Go into hiding where no one can find her. Then she asked me how much money I could give her."

"Did you give her some?" asked Sue.

"I gave her what I had here, about $600, money I had been saving up from tips, mostly in small bills. She told me she had a credit card that would keep her going for a while."

"How about her son?" asked Sue.

"I took him over to a friend's house so he wouldn't hear this conversation. He's used to staying with me. This has happened a lot over the years, so he won't think much about it. He's got his own bedroom here, I'll take him to school and look after him. Life will go on almost as usual."

"Did Molly give you any indication of where she might be going?" asked Ray.

"No. She had a destination she didn't want to share with me. She said she'd call from time to time to check in. That's all I can tell you, Sheriff."

'Do you know anything about Molly being involved with a church?" asked Sue.

"Oh, that church. That's become so important to her. She never was much interested in religion until she got involved with that church. Lots of times Scott ends up staying here because she's got church activities. I don't know, something doesn't seem quite right about it. Maybe she was just sneaking off to spend the night with Richard."

Ray slowly stood up, "Thank you for telling us all this. It's been very helpful."

"Is she in danger, real danger?" Birchard asked.

"She may be. But we're doing our best to get to the bottom of this mystery. We hope to get it resolved before anyone else is harmed," said Ray.

41

After returning to Sue's Jeep, they sat for a long moment, each reflecting on what they had just heard. Finally, Sue turned the ignition switch, the sound of the engine ending the silence.

"What now, kimosabe?" asked Sue as she began backing out of the drive.

"I think we need to talk to Rod Gunne again. He seems to be at the center of this. Why don't you turn around, we'll start at the church and then check Gunne's residence."

"Ray," started Sue, as she continued driving north, "it's almost six. I don't think anything is going to happen tonight that would be prevented by our trying to track down Gunne. But if you still want to do that after I drop you off, go for it. I'm going to pick up Simone and go to my yoga class. I haven't been there in weeks." She paused, glanced at Ray briefly, and continued. "And after, maybe I will go and have a few glasses of wine with the girls. Ray, I need a bit of normalcy. I can't continue to work sixteen hours a day. And you can't either. We're burning out. Both of us."

Ray started to respond, carefully forming his opening sentence before he gave voice to it. He caught himself at the last moment and remained silent. He looked over at his colleague; he could see that she was exhausted. For months she had been at his side during several grueling murder investigations, selflessly working nights and weekends without ever a complaint. It slowly began to sink in. Sue was emotionally and physically drained. She was teetering on the edge of total burnout, a state from which people wander away from once rewarding jobs to seek something new.

Then he thought, *Maybe I'm projecting*, he thought, but he couldn't deny his own feelings of weariness. As he sat there reflecting on what was going on with Sue, Ray realized that he was having difficulty keeping the wall in place that provided the emotional distance necessary to work effectively. For months most of his energy had been focused on work. He had made little time for his friends and was probably responsible for the seemingly sudden end to his relationship with Sarah.

After Sue dropped Ray off, he returned to his office and keyed his notes from the conversation with Ruth Birchard. He thought about Molly. She probably had the information to help quickly break this case. *Why did she choose to do a runner rather than coming to them for help?* he muttered out loud. He thought about how wary and apprehensive she seemed during their interviews. Given what Ruth Birchard had told them, Molly must have developed a deep-seated fear of law enforcement during her many years of using illicit drugs. He wondered how many weeks she had stayed clean to pass her employment medical test, and if and when she had returned to using drugs.

By the time Ray drove up his drive, covered with a fresh dusting of lake-effect snow, it was dark, and he was tired and hungry. He stood at his kitchen counter for several minutes and sorted the mail, noting that there were two *New Yorkers*. He checked the dates, curiously there were two consecutive weeks.

Without energy or imagination, he made a supper of bread, cheese, and an apple, washing it down with several mugs of chamomile tea.

As he ate, his attention was focused on a long article in the *New Yorker* on a conflict of people and values in a rural area of New Jersey little more than twenty-five miles from Manhattan. Ray took interest in the fact that some of the problems discussed in the article were similar to those he faced in northern Michigan, the often-conflicting interests of the locals and the more affluent part-time residents.

Later, standing at his writing desk, pen in hand and his journal open before him, Ray mentally reviewed the day. Much of his first few paragraphs was a recapitulation of his thoughts as Sue drove him back to the office. He wrote about what he perceived was going on with her, and how he was probably experiencing much of the same feelings. They were both being worn down by the workload and the trauma of the two horrific murders. He sympathized with Sue's need for a life and was forced to confront how the demands of his job and his own workaholic tendencies were keeping him from the companionship and support of his friends. Ray stopped writing for a while and thought about his life. He had given up a career in college teaching to return to the area that he loved. And in the early years as sheriff, he had taken the time to walk the beaches, watch the setting sun, and kayak the big lake. He had skied in the winter, walked the streams with a fly rod in the summer, spent time with good friends, and struggled with romance. Now he seldom did any of those things. He wondered how and when he could get some balance back in his life.

Ray started flipping through the notebook, moving back weeks, then months. The name *Elise Lovell* pulled his attention. He scanned his entry from November where he commented on his interview with her during the early inquiries in the Lynne Boyd shooting. He noted her perceptiveness, wondering how much of that came from her training as psychiatric social worker and how much of it was just an innate trait. Ray stopped and read the entry a second time, he mouthed, psychiatric social worker. He thought about his most recent encounter with Elise. Hadn't she told him and Sue that she was a chemist by training? Maybe she did chemistry and changed majors, he thought. But he suddenly had a feeling something was very wrong.

He grabbed his phone and started to call Sue, stopping at the last instant. It would have to wait till morning.

42

Ray was well into his workday, his attention focused on the necessary bureaucratic tasks of his job, when his secretary, Jan, popped in to relay a message from Sue. She was taking a half-day of personal leave and would see him in the afternoon. He was a bit startled by the news. He had never known Sue to take leave time during an important investigation.

They had both been working intensively for months without a respite. And one of the things that he had noticed early in her tenure with the department was that Sue seemed to share his work orientation. In the past, one of the women he dated had accused him of being a workaholic on her way out of the relationship. But now as he thought back on it, that assertion was probably true, his life revolved around his work. He sat confronting the fact that he had not been sensitive to Sue's needs. At her age she should be pursuing some of the other things that life offers.

Ray began to wonder if Sue was in the process of starting to look for another job. Given her background, experience, and skill, Sue could move downstate or out-of-state and greatly improve her salary and get a normal workweek. He remembered that she had also expressed an interest in graduate school, and perhaps even a career change. She had also talked about finding a man and starting a family. With a sense of uneasiness, Ray focused on the tasks at hand.

A few hours later, when Sue came in, Ray noted how rested and relaxed she looked. She seemed more like the personality that he had
become used to, easy-going and usually good-humored.

"Anything happening?" she asked.

"Quiet morning," said Ray. "No new bodies or suspicious fires." He
reflected on what he said and thought he should lighten the tone. "Just
another day in paradise."

"Good," Sue responded. "I could really get into that routine for a
while. Searching for lost dogs and doing elementary school traffic
safety talks never looked better."

"I did have a thought, however," said Ray. "Remember the first time
we talked to Elise Lovell when Lynne Boyd was shot?"

"Yes," said Sue. "Talk about crunchy granola. She was so perfectly
turned out in clothes made of natural fibers. And her make-up was im-
peccable. It was sort of Woodstock does Vogue. And it was fun to watch
you."

"Why's that?"

"You seemed to be so taken with her then. I don't know if I've ever
seen anything quite like it. And she certainly was aware of what she was
doing and how to work you."

"What are you talking about?" asked Ray.

"Trust me, Ray. She was working you like, well, I don't know quite
like what. But she had your full attention. In fact, it got me to thinking
about the women you choose. They tend to be professional, brainy, and
readers. And I'm not saying that Elise isn't bright, not at all. But she
doesn't seem your type. I was surprised that you seemed to be totally
attracted to her, whether you were aware of it or not."

"I think you're imagining things," Ray retorted.

"No," said Sue. "That was the beauty of it all. She was so skilled at
working you and you were totally unaware of what was going on. Trust
me on this. It's a woman thing."

"Why didn't you mention something at the time?"

"It didn't seem necessary. She was providing information that confirmed what we both believed to be true. Although you did a better job
than me, neither of us was able to overcome our dislike of Dirk Lowther.
That said, what Elise told us in no way changed the course of the investigation. And," Sue chuckled, "it gave me some new insight into your

character. It made you a bit more human. You could very occasionally be something other than totally cognitive and objective. That's a good thing, Ray. It's okay to be human." Sue paused briefly. "I think I got us off track. What were you going to tell me about Elise Lovell?"

"That first interview during the Lynne Boyd shooting investigation," said Ray, "Elise suggested that she had some professional insight into the matter, given her training as a clinical psychologist. Do you remember that?"

"Yes," Sue answered. "And then she told us what Lynne had shared with her about her marriage. Elise further explained her own observations of Dirk. She seemed very insightful."

"But when we recently talked to her about Brenda Manton," said Ray, "she told us that she was a chemist. Did you catch that?"

"Yes."

"Doesn't that bother you?" asked Ray.

"No, I thought that somewhere along the line she had college work in chemistry. Perhaps it was an undergraduate minor, maybe even a major. And later, when she started to think about graduate school, she decided to go in a different direction. If I went back, I might do something in art."

"So that never bothered you?" said Ray.

"No, and I'm not sure it means anything, but perhaps we should check it out."

"I think we should. So would you get in contact with Elise Lovell. See if you can set up another interview. And maybe you could start doing a background check on her."

"I'll get on it right away," said Sue.

"While you're doing that, I'm going to go out and talk to Rod Gunne again. He seems to be at the center of so much of this. Let's plan on meeting late this afternoon." Ray looked at her and smiled, "Four, Sue, not seven or eight. We'll compare notes and decide what to do next. And we will complete our work day at five."

43

As Ray entered the central revolving door of The Church for the Next Millennium, he stopped for a minute, allowing his eyes to adjust from the sun light and snow-covered terrain to the more subdued illumination of the building's interior.

"How can I direct you?" came a deep resonant voice.

Ray focused on a figure at the side of the door, a large man in a blue sport coat and gray pants. They carefully eyed one another.

Private security, thought Ray, "*and not local, but professional and expensive.*"

"May I direct you, sir?" the man asked again.

"I know where I'm going," answered Ray with authority as he marched toward Gunne's office. He found Gunne's secretary working at a computer keyboard.

"May I help you?" she asked.

"I'm here to see Mr. Gunne."

"Is he expecting you, Sheriff?" she asked, looking up over her glasses.

"I would like to see him now."

She picked up her phone, set it back in the cradle and said, "Excuse me a minute. I'll see if he's available." As she walked toward Gunne's office, Ray followed her, pushing past her after she opened the door.

"Excuse the interruption," she said, her eyes moving from Gunne to Ray. She quickly withdrew, closing the door behind her.

"We need to talk," said Ray. Gunne pushed the laptop that he had been working on to the side and stood. Ray could see a spreadsheet on the screen.

"Sheriff, would you please have a seat. I can have Shirley bring us some coffee."

"Mr. Gunne, I'd like you to sit right there," said Ray pointing to a chair. I don't want a desk between us." He positioned his chair before sitting so they were directly across from each other.

"How can I help you, Sheriff?"

"You can start by telling me everything that you know," said Ray.

"I'm sorry. I don't quite follow."

"Brenda Manton worked on your church, she ends up dead. Richard Kinver has worked for you and is a member of your congregation. Now he's dead. Molly Birchard, Brenda's best friend and one of your flock has disappeared. And you live in a house that belongs to an elderly couple, and no one seems to know where they are."

"I don't understand, Sheriff. I've been devastated by the deaths of two very good people, but what does that have to do with me?"

"That's exactly what I'm trying to find out."

Gunne remained silent; he stared at Ray. Then he said, "Am I under suspicion or a person of interest or whatever phrase is used in police jargon?"

"Not at this time," said Ray, "but you have had contact with all of these people. And I want to know what you know. Perhaps you can help us get to the bottom of things." Ray pulled a small notebook from an inside pocket and opened it. He peered at his notes. "Earlier you told me that you had no personal relationship with Brenda Manton. Is that still your story?"

"Personal relationship, what do you mean by that?" Gunne responded.

"Let's not quibble. I think you know exactly what I mean by that."

"Like I think that I told you before, Brenda Manton was one of many craftsmen and artisans who worked on this building. In the course of the design of the artwork and getting it installed, we developed a friendship. For several months we worked together very closely. And it's true, I didn't have that kind of relationship with most of the people on the job, like plumbers and electricians. But I am sure, Sheriff, you understand the difference. Brenda's work was creative. I had a loose concept of what I wanted the walls to look like. There was a lot of going back and forth to attain the look and feel that I desired for this building."

"I understand that," said Ray. "But this relationship seems to have extended beyond the bounds of a normal professional relationship." He looked at his notes. "For example, you told me that you visited Brenda's home several times to look at designs. Did you ever visit her then or later as a social occasion, to have a glass of wine, to chat, something more personal?"

"Like I told you, Sheriff, our relationship was professional, nothing more, never."

"So you never had sex with her, then, did you?"

"No," said Gunne, straightening the crease on one leg of his pants.

"Tell me about this house you're living in."

"I'm renting it," said Gunne.

"How did you learn about this property?"

"I was talking to Richard Kinver. I told him I was looking for a rental, someplace I could live for six months while I was looking for a place to buy. He told me he had a home that would be ideal for my needs. He said he was the caretaker of this property for some absentee owners and that he could get me a good rental rate for the winter months."

"So you never met the owners?" said Ray.

"No."

"To whom did you pay the rent?"

"I paid Richard Kinver. He picked up the rent first of each month."

"And how much was the rent?"

"It was $2000."

"$2000, that's a lot of money. But for a piece of property worth millions, quite modest. Did you think that was peculiar?"

"Sheriff, I thought I was getting a deal. Richard told me that they were two elderly people who had more money than they could ever use."

"So you never met them?"

"No, never."

"Did you have any other business dealings with Richard Kinver?"

"He did most of the excavation work on the new building. He also helped with landscaping. And this winter he's been clearing the parking lots."

"Had he become part of your congregation?"

"Yes. His personal life seemed to be in chaos. I think through my ministry he was beginning to take control of his destiny."

Ray changed direction. "Elise Lovell." He just let the name hang and waited for a response.

"Brenda Manton's assistant, what about her?"

"She was around a lot when the construction was going on, wasn't she?"

"Yes. She and Brenda worked together very closely. They seemed almost inseparable. In fact, and I don't usually talk about these things, I was wondering if something could have been going on between them, if you get my drift."

"Did you develop a friendship with her?"

"No."

"Did she come to your church?"

"I see her in the congregation from time to time. I wouldn't say that she attends on a regular basis."

"And you never had a personal relationship with her?"

"No, Sheriff, never. And I hope you can see from this, by my answers, that I have had limited contact with these people and that my relationships have always been of a proper nature."

"That appears to be the case, Mr. Gunne."

"It is the case, Sheriff. I assure you. This is all very tragic. These were good people. And if there's anything I can do to help your investigation, please let me know."

"Well," said Ray, "there is one thing. Would you be willing to come to the office and take a polygraph?"

Gunne was slow in responding. Finally he asked, "I would do that. When?"

"Tomorrow morning at nine o'clock. Just come to the main desk at our office and someone will make sure you get to the right place." Ray stood and shook hands with Gunne, wondering if he would really show up.

44

When Ray returned to the County Center, he saw Sue at the far end of the parking lot with Simone tethered on a long lead. After parking, he walked over to join her.

"No daycare today?" he asked as Simone ran to greet him.

"No daycare this week or next," said Sue. "They've gone to Florida, said they needed a break from March in Michigan. How was his eminence, the Reverend Mister Gunne?"

"He affirmed again that he knows nothing about anything," said Ray, picking up the wiggling terrier and absorbing a couple affectionate licks to the right cheek.

"I thought you'd find a way to squeeze him a bit."

"He's coming in for a polygraph tomorrow at 9:00," said Ray, as he returned Simone to the ground.

"Cool," said Sue as they walked back toward the office. "How did you do that?"

"I let him tell me all of his contacts with Manton, Kinver, and our Molly were strictly professional. Then I offered the opportunity for a polygraph." Ray held the door for Sue and Simone. After they got to his office, with the door shut, Sue asked, "What does your gut tell you about Gunne?"

"He probably is not responsible for the crimes, but he's no innocent. Right now he's doing his best to distance himself from these events. He is in full protection mode. I'm sure a scandal wouldn't be good for business. How did you do?" Ray asked.

"Interesting afternoon. First of all I attempted to call Elise Lovell. It appears that the Lovell landline has been disconnected, so I thought I'd drop by the house. They have this cute little place in the village close to the bay. It's an old Victorian cottage, quite small, and beautifully restored. But the place appears to be empty. So I went next door and talked to the neighbor, a Mrs. Clara Galbraith. She says she remembers you as a little boy and says that she was a friend of your mother's from church."

"Clara Galbraith," said Ray, "I think I remember her. I'm not sure."

"Well, she's a real chatty Cathy. Once you pull the string you can't get her to shut up. Her hearing is probably mostly gone. It was difficult for me to get her to listen to my questions."

"So did you learn anything?"

"I learned that this is a person you don't want to live next to, even if you live the most exemplary life. She seems to spend most of the day watching everything that happens in the neighborhood. When I was finally able to get a few questions in, I learned that Joe Lovell has taken a one-semester teaching job at a small private college in Ohio. She said Joe told her that he hoped that it would lead to a full-time position. He and the kids made the move there in late January."

"How about Elise?"

"Clara said that she sees Elise occasionally. That she was continuing to live in the area to keep her business going and supposedly making trips to Ohio on an irregular basis. Clara made it clear she didn't understand this. A mother's place was with her children. And then she launched into a long discussion about Elise and her lifestyle. It was hard for me to sort things out. In addition to being hard of hearing, I think the old dear is a bit dotty, also."

"So you're sort of stalled," said Ray.

"No, not really. When I got back to the office I started a computer search. Elise Lovell does not pop up on any of the usual databases, no arrests under that name. So then I was wondering about her maiden name. The Internet is really wonderful. I found her wedding listed in her sorority newsletter, complete with her maiden name and hometown. Remember in our first interview with her, she mentioned that her husband had taught at Northern Illinois University. It appears that she was a student there also, at least as an undergraduate."

"So did she study both chemistry and psychology?" ask Ray.

"That's still a mystery," said Sue. "I haven't found the right sources for that yet. But finding her home town was very helpful."

"Let me guess, you got into the archive of her hometown paper and got lots of information."

"I'm not sure there's a local paper. She's from a small town in northwestern Illinois. I did talk to the sole detective in the local police department, a woman. She was very cagey and not forthcoming. I had to explain to her the case we're working on and that Elise Lovell, nee Brickston, who grew up in her town, was one of many individuals whose background we are looking into. She told me she couldn't talk about juvenile records that had been sealed by the court. And that almost sounded like the end of it. But then she said that if I showed up in person with suitable identification, she would steer me in the right direction."

"We need to figure out how to get you there," said Ray.

Sue chuckled. "Well, I know that the department has a ban on any unnecessary travel, but I have a reservation for the seven o'clock flight to Chicago. I'll pick up a rental there and drive the rest of the way. With your permission, of course."

"I'll find the money somewhere," said Ray.

"There's one more thing," said Sue, pointing to Simone, who was curled up and asleep in the one overstuffed chair in the office. "You'd have to look after her, but she's really not much trouble. Just some food and water and a walk now and then. She goes to the door and makes a command bark. She's very good at letting you know what she needs. Also, she will want to share your pillow. I hope you're not averse to that." Sue sat down a brown paper bag on the desk. "Here's a supply of food for Simone, give her half a can at night and in the morning. She's a bit of a picky eater, I'm afraid," Sue added. "I should be only gone a day, two at the most. I've got to pack, and get to the airport. Brett is going to drive me."

"You'll keep me in the loop?"

"Yes. Which means that you have to keep your cell phone charged, Ray. That's the number I'll call you on."

45

As Ray started to unload the groceries, Simone sat on the floor near him. Her bright black eyes fixed on his every movement. He glanced down at her. "Do you want your dinner?" he asked. Simone wagged her tail and emitted a sharp little bark.

"You have to wait a few minutes until I get the groceries put away." Ray continued to work at sorting and storing the contents of two large bags. And Simone held her position, waiting expectantly.

Finally, he turned his attention to Simone's dinner. He pulled one of the cans of dog food from the brown paper sack and set it on the counter. He retrieved an opener from a drawer and opened the can. He lifted the lid away and looked at the contents; then he smelled them. Peering down at Simone, he said, "No wonder you're a picky eater." Then he tossed the can into the garbage.

"How about a lamb chop and some rice?" he asked. Simone wagged her tail again and barked several times enthusiastically.

"How much language do you have?" he asked. "Are you responding to what I say, or just the tone that I'm using?"

Simone held her position, looking directly at Ray with an inscrutable expression.

"Well, either way, lamb and rice has got to be a lot better than dog food."

Ray started some rice, prepared a salad, and laid out four lamb chops on a broiler pan. He was about to put them in the oven when he saw a white and yellow sea kayak glide by the window. He opened the door and Hannah Jeffers came in, dressed in a dry suit and carrying a backpack.

Before he could say anything, Hannah blurted, "Boy, do I have a lot to tell you, but I'm soaking wet under this dry suit and totally chilled. Would you make me something warm to drink while I'm changing?"

"What do you want, tea, coffee, something else?"

"Anything, Ray. As long as it's hot. Who is your friend?" asked Hannah, noticing the dog for the first time.

"That's Simone. She's a houseguest for a day or two. We were just about to have dinner. Would you like to join us?"

"Never turn down a meal, especially if it looks like a good one," responded Hannah as she headed off to change her clothes.

Ray started a kettle of water to boil, the second salad, and added more lamb chops to the broiler pan. Hannah emerged from the guest room wearing jeans, a black turtleneck, and a red fleece jacket.

"Feeling better?" Ray asked.

"Lots, but I still need a hot drink."

"The water is hot. I can make you coffee, tea…"

"How about some tea, herbal, with lots of honey."

Ray pulled several boxes from a drawer and set them on the counter. He set out two mugs and a bottle of honey. "Pick your poison," he said, pointing to the boxes of tea. "How do you like your lamb chops?"

"Not too pink. Do you have any mint jelly?" she asked.

Ray gave her a long look.

"Guess that was a *faux pas*," said Hannah with a chuckle.

"You said you have something to tell me."

"Yes," Hannah answered. "When we were kayaking together you mentioned in passing that you were looking for a rather eccentric character who sometimes camps out in the caves on the shelf ice."

"Yes," said Ray. "His name is Tristan Laird. He may hold the key to solving at least one of the murder cases we've been working on."

"He didn't give me his name," said Hannah, "but I think I met the character you're talking about. He's probably mid-to-late 30s, looks like he's been living in the wild for a while. Not very communicative. Reminds me of someone who smoked way too much dope or perhaps had some kind of traumatic brain injury."

"I think you may have found him," said Ray. "When and where did you meet up with him?"

"I launched in the same place we did before and followed the creek out beyond the shelf ice. Instead of going north, I headed south. Two or 3 miles out I found a number of large ice caves. I was having fun playing around. I would paddle in at a good rate and see how far I could get into a cave and then slide back out again. On the fourth or fifth cave I paddled into I was surprised to find someone. In fact I was rather frightened at first. I tried to back out, but got stuck. And then he grabbed my boat and pulled me in farther. He wanted to know who I was and why I was there. He seemed pretty paranoid."

"Then what happened?" said Ray.

"I popped my spray skirt and got out of the boat." Hannah looked over his shoulder. "Is something burning?" she asked.

Ray pulled the pan of lamb chops from under the broiler and set it on the top of the stove. "I don't think you'll find these too pink. Then what happened?" he asked.

"We had a conversation of sorts. Initially I did almost all the talking. Eventually he started answering some of my questions. He's very laconic, very frightened."

"So what did you learn?" asked Ray, growing impatient.

"He told me he was hiding out, that someone was after him. And he's unwell, Ray. He looks malnourished, and he's doing a lot of coughing. I suspect he's got pneumonia. I explained to him that I was a doctor and that he appeared to be sick, that he needed medical attention. He had a kayak in the cave with him, a skin-on-frame. I told him if he came with me I would get him medical care and make sure that he was safe. No dice. He's too frightened."

"Then what?" asked Ray.

"Well, I finally got him to admit that he was sick. I told him I would come back tomorrow with some medicine. I wanted to come in the morning, but he asked me to come in the afternoon. He said he usually sleeps on shore.

"So this is what we agreed upon," continued Hannah, "I would meet him at two in the same location if the lake was flat like today. And I told him that I wanted to bring another doctor with me, that I was a heart surgeon, and I wanted someone who might better be able to help him with this problem. He didn't want to hear about that, not at all, but I think in the end I had convinced him that it was necessary."

"And what if the lake isn't flat?"

"Then all bets are off," said Hannah. "Are you ready to practice medicine without a license?"

"What do you have in mind?" asked Ray.

"I can make a rough diagnosis about what he needs. I mean, it would be better to have him in the hospital, but I'll do my best given the circumstances. And I think we should take him a dry sleeping bag, some clothes, and a supply of freeze-dried food. I'll also pack some meds. While we are with him, perhaps you can get some information from him. Or perhaps we can get him to come with us. I think we'll just have to play it by ear. Like I said, he should be in a hospital for diagnostic work, and then spend some time in a suitable environment for recovery." She looked at Ray, "How does it sound?"

Ray was silent for a long moment. Finally he said, "This will be real challenging. But thank you for remembering. This could be the break we've been looking for."

"Have you met him before? Might he recognize you?"

"I've never had any contact with him. That said, I'm out there." Ray paused, "I've got a cold weather neoprene hood, only has openings for my eyes, nose, and mouth. You don't see much of my face. That should work. If it doesn't, we'll deal."

Ray looked at the food he had been preparing. "We better eat. Everything is getting cold."

"How about Simone?" Hannah asked.

"Would you chop up one of these lamb chops and mix it with some of the rice for Simone, and I'll get the rest of the meal on the table."

"When you return her to her owner, she'll never want to eat dog food again."

"Everyone has got troubles," chuckled Ray.

46

At eight sharp the next morning Bob Taft, the polygraph examiner, dressed in a carefully pressed blue shirt and tan corduroys was at Ray's office. Bob had retired to the region more than a decade before, and now worked as an independent contractor to police agencies around the state. He knocked on the door frame before entering.

"Morning," said Ray, looking away from his screen. "Come on in. Can I get you some coffee?"

"I'll have a cup with you," answered Taft. "Who's curled up over there, your new deputy?"

"That's Simone. It's a long story, but for the near term Sue Lawrence has accepted guardianship for her. And Sue is in Illinois today as part of this investigation, so I'm looking after the dog."

"I want to go over that email you sent me last night," said Taft. "And thank you for that. So many departments don't give me sufficient background and then expect that I work miracles for them."

They settled at the conference table, Ray pouring coffee into mugs from an insulated carafe. Ray gave Taft, a retired police officer from suburban Detroit and a respected polygraph examiner, an overview of the Manton murder and the Kinver murder. Then he explained that while there was nothing that connected Rod Gunne directly to either of these crimes, Gunne knew and had dealings with both of the victims.

"So, he's told me, Bob, that his only contact with Manton was when she was creating and installing some of her work in his new church. He insists that there was never any personal relationship. I want to know if he's telling the truth about that. And then I want to know if he has any suspicions or knowledge about who might have killed Brenda Manton. And finally, obviously, I want to know if he was in any way directly or indirectly connected with this crime. The same thing with the Kinver murder. He is a very polished character, and I suspect you'll find a fair amount of hubris there as well. Do you have any questions?"

"I don't think so. Given what you've just told me, your e-mail, and some questions I worked up last evening, I think I'm in pretty good shape. I just need a quiet place to get these questions revised. I should be ready to go by nine."

"Do you need a printer?"

"I can just read things off the screen of my laptop. Thanks. It sounds like I will have an interesting morning," said Taft. He smiled at Ray. "Usual place?" he asked.

"Yes," said Ray, coming to his feet. "I'll help you set up."

Returning to his office, Ray phoned Sue Lawrence.

"Ray, you remembered to charge your cell phone?"

"No, actually I forgot. I'm plugging it in right now, hold on a minute. Okay, I'm back. Are you there yet?"

"Ray, I'm in Illinois, central time, I'm having breakfast at the hotel. The plane was late departing, weather problems. I didn't get to O'Hare until close to 10 o'clock our time. And it was after 11 by the time I picked up a rental and found the motel. I'll be on the road pretty soon. Anything happening at your end?"

"I think I may finally meet Tristan Laird today." Ray explained his conversation with Hannah Jeffers the previous evening and laid out the plan for meeting Laird in the afternoon.

"Amazing," said Sue. "This might be the breakthrough we are looking for. I'll pray for flat water so Tristan will show up."

"Me, too," said Ray. "I hope I can get some information from him without scaring him off."

"How's Simone. Is she eating for you?"

"No problem, but she did try to hog my pillow most of the night."

Ray could hear Sue chuckling. "That's one of her more endearing qualities. It means she really likes you. I've got to run, Ray. I'll keep in touch."

"Good," he responded, ending the call.

Ray did his best to focus on paperwork, but his thoughts were elsewhere. He wanted to be a fly on the wall, watching Bob Taft slowly leading Rod Gunne through a carefully developed line of questioning. Then his thoughts flashed to the afternoon. He wondered if he would get any information from Tristan Laird. And he wondered if there might be any way to coax Laird into getting needed medical attention. How could he offer him protection without tipping his hat that he was really a police officer, not a doctor?

He took Simone for a long walk around the parking lot. She took her time, sniffing at the brownish grass near the edge of the pavement that had been exposed by the snowplow. Finally he returned to his office and forced himself to work through a pile of paper.

It was after 11 o'clock when Bob Taft appeared in Ray's office. "How did it go?" asked Ray.

"He's an interesting man," Taft responded with his calm smile, a trait that put his subjects at ease and helped make him such an effective examiner. "We covered a lot of territory. It will take me a while to type up a complete report for you."

"And I have to scoot out of here pretty soon. I've got something going on this afternoon to get ready for. But give me the high points. That would really help," said Ray.

Taft settled at the conference table and opened his laptop. "I'll start with the major questions first," he said. "Rod Gunne was probably not the killer in either of these cases. Did he have something more than a professional relationship with Brenda Manton? Yes. Did he have sex with her? Yes. Was he in or near her home the evening she was killed? No. Did he have any suspicions of who might have killed her? He answered no on this, but he probably wasn't telling the truth."

"How sure are you of these results?" asked Ray.

"Very," Taft responded. "The man is smooth with great social skills. He's a veteran liar. That said, he was the perfect candidate. There aren't many gray areas in his chart, it was obvious when he was lying.

"How about Richard Kinver's murder?"

"It doesn't appear that he had anything to do with that, and he had no direct knowledge of the crime. When I asked him if he had any suspicions as to the perp, he said no, but his body was telling the machine something else."

"How about Elise Lovell?" asked Ray.

"He was uncomfortable with this line of questioning. It appears that he had a personal relationship with her, sex included."

"And Molly Birchard?"

"The same. Seems like the reverend is spreading more than just the gospel," he added with a playful smile.

"He's created his own gospel," said Ray. "It's about 2 1/2 standard deviations south of any mainline religion. When will I have a written report?"

"I'll send you a quick summary later today. The complete document with all the supporting information, more than anyone ever wants to know, will take a few days."

"Sorry that we can't do lunch today, I've got to leave in a few minutes," said Ray. "I really enjoy our conversations. Let's get together soon. And thank you for coming in on short notice."

"Happy to do it, Ray. I'll be interested to hear how this case turns out."

47

After carrying their kayaks to the stream, Ray and Hannah Jeffers sorted through their gear bags, attaching some items—their cell phones protected in small transparent dry bags and their bilge pumps—under the bungees in front of the cockpits and stuffing other things into the pockets of their life jackets. Ray handed Hannah a guide vest, a black net affair with five large pockets, four in the front and one in the back, constructed of black nylon mesh.

"I'd like to have everything that we might need initially on us. I'll put the sleeping bag and extra clothing in my rear hatch and you can carry the food in yours," he said, pulling a similar vest over his life jacket.

"Do you have room for this?" he asked, holding out a small flare gun, an orange plastic pistol with three extra 12 gauge shells. "I want each of us carrying the same safety gear. Have you ever fired a pistol?" Ray asked.

Hannah laughed, "You're talking to an infantry officer." She looked again closely, "So it's loaded, and I release this safety and pull the trigger?"

"You got it," said Ray. "A piece of simple, crude technology that is very dependable. Here's one more thing to put on your deck." Ray handed her two wooden dowels with steel spikes driven into one end, connected by a rope at the opposite ends.

"What's that for?" she asked.

"Fishermen carry these when they are on the ice. If you happen to come out of your boat, you can pull yourself up on the ice."

"Cool. Time for an equipment check?" asked Hannah.

"Sure, radios on and working, tow belts in place, and we've got all your medical gear in our vests."

They climbed into their kayaks and attached the tight fitting, neoprene spray skirts around the cockpit combings. Seal-like, they slid down the ice-covered bank into the stream and paddled out onto the lake.

"A bit of a chop," Hannah observed. "I thought it was supposed to be flat."

"The NOAA forecast called for waves up to two feet early on, with a storm coming in this evening."

"I hope Tristan felt well enough to venture out. He's not in good shape," Hannah observed.

"Lead the way," said Ray as they turned south. "About how far do we need to go?"

"I should have paid more attention to that," she answered, sounding somewhat abashed. "And I wasn't carrying a GPS. But it's down there at the end of the bay in the tallest area of the ice shelf. That's where I found the biggest caves."

They paddled away from the shore on a direct line toward that section of shelf ice. As they neared the area, Ray asked, "Where should we start looking for the cave?"

"Right about there," Hannah pointed with her paddle and led the way.

After they worked their way through more than a dozen caves she observed, "They all look pretty much alike, but it was in here somewhere, and I don't think it could have been much farther." A few dozen yards farther she peered into the largest cave they had encountered. "This is it," she said.

Hannah turned her bow toward the opening of the cave and paddled hard. Her momentum carried her boat about half way up on the ice. Ray watched as a thin figure emerged from the dark interior and pulled her boat completely out of the water. After she was out of her cockpit and facing him, Ray followed suit, his kayak ending up behind hers.

Hannah grabbed the bow handle on his boat and pulled it out of the water at the side of her boat.

"Watch your footing," she cautioned as Ray started to climb out of his cockpit.

Tristan Laird was huddled in the back of the cave, surrounded by clothing and a damp-looking sleeping bag. A small, hand-built kayak was pushed up against the wall of the cave.

Hannah went to Tristan's side, pulling on a headlamp. "This is my friend," she said, moving her head toward Ray. "He's going to assist me."

Tristan kept his eyes on Hannah, not overtly acknowledging Ray's presence.

"When did you paddle in this morning?" she asked.

"Stayed here, too weak," Laird answered in a weak, breathy tone.

Ray knelt at Laird's other side.

"First I need to get your temperature," she said, removing a small electronic thermometer from a vest pocket. She slid it under his tongue, and they sat in silence for a few minutes. Hannah carefully removed the device from his mouth, and she focused her headlamp on the digital readout.

"Tristan, I've got to listen to your chest. We'll try not to undress you too much, I know how cold it is in here."

With Ray's help, she unzipped Laird's down jacket and the second fleece jacket under it. She slid the chest piece of the stethoscope up under his t-shirt, instructing him to take deep breaths as she listened to his lungs, first on his back and then on his chest. When she was finished, they carefully zipped him back into his jackets.

Ray looked across at Hannah. He could see by her expression that Laird's condition was serious. He imagined that she was trying to figure out a way to convince Laird that he needed the kind of care that could only be provided in a hospital.

"How am I, Doc?" he asked in a wheezy voice.

"Things aren't good, Tristan. You have a lot of congestion in your lungs and a high fever. You need to be in a hospital."

"You were going to bring me meds," said Tristan in a pleading tone.

"I did, Tristan. Meds and food and a dry sleeping bag. But you're too sick for them to do you much good. My colleague here," she gestured toward Ray, "will confirm my diagnosis."

"It's true," said Ray in a soft voice. "We can save your life if we can quickly get you to a hospital."

"I can't leave. Someone is trying to kill me."

"We'll get you safely out of here to a place where you can get better," said Hannah.

"We can get round-the-clock protection, no one will be able to get you," added Ray.

"Just leave the meds and food. I'll be okay," he pleaded.

"Tristan," said Ray, leaning close. "The weather is changing, the wind is coming up. You can hear it, can't you?" He paused to let the sound of the wind and waves echo through the cave. "Six to eight foot waves tonight. This cave is going to be flooded. If we are going to get you out safely, we've got to leave now."

"I'm too weak. I can't paddle."

"If you can sit in your boat, we can tow you back. I'll radio for assistance and have an ambulance and police waiting for us."

Laird offered feeble resistance as they lifted him by his arms and moved him toward his boat. They carefully helped him pull on a spray skirt and PFD. Then they maneuvered his less than limber body into the tight-fitting cockpit.

"How are we going to do this?" asked Sue.

"It's a tippy little kayak, and he's very weak. We can't take a chance on him capsizing. Why don't you ramp with him, and I'll tow."

"It's a long way."

"When I get tired we'll change off. Let me call dispatch and get people rolling, then we'll launch."

After Ray called for assistance, he got into his boat and carefully slid out of the cave. He waited as Hannah slowly pushed Laird's boat in his direction. With one arm, he held onto the second boat while pushing away from the ice with his paddle, making room for Hannah to launch. Once she was on the water, she ramped up with Laird. Ray hooked his towline to the bow of her boat and paddled away slowly, allowing the rope to spool out of the bag. Once it was taut, he began to paddle, slowly at first to get the other boats moving, then adding more power, his eyes fixed on a distant destination. He settled into a steady rhythm, trying to set a rate that he could maintain for the entire route. Minutes crept by. Ray could feel the sweat begin to build in the interior of his dry suit. He kept looking back to check on the other boats.

Ray focused on moving as quickly as possible toward their destination. He was startled by the sharp report of a pistol. As he turned he saw a dark figure standing near the end of the shelf ice, firing toward the kayaks that were bouncing in waves at the end of his towline. Then he saw a flash from Hannah's flare gun, the blaze of magnesium hitting the center of the figure, followed by an explosion of flames as the bulky nylon jacket of the shooter was ignited by the white-hot projectile. He heard a scream and then saw the shooter plunge into rolling surf.

Ray raced back, "Are you hit?"

"No," Hannah answered. "We're both okay."

Ray let the towline go slack and paddled over to the edge of the shelf ice in the area where he saw the body hit the lake. He maneuvered back and forth several times in the reflecting waves, peering into the dark water. Then, pulling the GPS off his deck, he set a waypoint.

"See anything?" Hannah asked.

"No. Must have gotten trapped under the ice. We'd better get going," Ray said, his destination now illuminated by the flashing lights of emergency vehicles. He got the slack out of the line and paddled toward their destination again, his efforts aided by the sudden burst of adrenalin.

48

Ray leaned against Hannah's Subaru and sipped on a water bottle one of the EMTs had given him before they left the scene with Tristan Laird, Hannah at Tristan's side attending to his needs. A pickup truck slowly came down the road in his direction and stopped a few yards in front of him. Ben Reilly gingerly opened the passenger's door and waved from the seat. A heavy black nylon jacket with his name and the department logo embroidered on the front was wrapped over his shoulders. Cut-off sweatpants covered the casted leg, with heavy socks and worn Birkenstocks on his feet.

"What are you doing here?" asked Ray.

"Couldn't keep him away," answered Maureen, Ben's wife, coming around the truck from the driver's side. "He calls Central Dispatch two or three times a day to see what's happening. He hasn't changed one bit."

"I was talking to Central when your call came in. I knew Sue was out of the area, and I thought you might need some help," Ben explained.

Ray looked toward Maureen who muttered, "It's alright. He needed to get out of the house."

"Ben, I could use your help. And he can do everything from here," Ray reassured Maureen. He retrieved his GPS from the driver's seat of Hannah's car. "Push this button to bring the display back on," he instructed. "When the dive team arrives, give them these coordinates. I think they'll be able to locate the body just under the ice shelf in that area. And Brett should soon be here to collect evidence and photograph the scene. He'll be able to figure it out from the coordinates too. I would bet the assailant's car is near. They probably followed us here. This is the closest open access. Maybe that black Audi," Ray pointed to a vehicle sitting at a plowed widening in the road.

"Do you have a name?" asked Ben, pulling a small notebook and pen from an interior pocket.

Ray took the notebook and pen, and using the top of the Subaru as a writing surface, carefully printed the first and last name. "I think that's who you will find," he said, handing back the notebook. "And you will probably find that name when you run the plates on that Audi."

"You okay?" asked Ben.

"You know how it is when you come off an adrenaline high. I just need to go slow for a bit. I'm going over to the medical center and check on things. Thank you for being here." Ray held Ben's hand, then gave Maureen a hug.

"You guys," she said. "You don't change."

Ray found Hannah Jeffers in the central area of the emergency wing, dressed in blue scrubs, standing at a desk keying information into a laptop.

"How's the patient?" he asked, lightly grasping her left elbow to indicate his presence.

As she turned and smiled, he could feel her exhaustion. "Things are under control. He's in the medical ICU, he'll have round-the-clock security. His name is not on the patient roster. No one will know that he's here."

"The prognosis?"

"Excellent. With treatment and proper nutrition, he'll be through the medical part quickly. Then there's the whole psychological side. He seems to need a minder."

"Brenda Manton, the first victim in this bizarre case, played that role in Tristan's life. I don't know who will do that now. I've heard that he has family somewhere out east. We'll try to contact them." Ray paused for a moment. "Will I be able to talk to Tristan anytime soon?"

"In a day or two, no problem. I know you will be attentive to his psy-chological state."

Ray nodded to show his comprehension of her statement. "I've got your car here."

"How about Simone?" Hannah asked.

"I forgot about her. She's probably okay. I hope."

"I better get you home fast. I hate seeing a sister in distress."

Ray led the way to the parking lot, tossing Hannah the keys across the hood of her car. They rode in silence most of the way. Finally she said, "It all happened so fast. I'm just starting to comprehend the enormity..." Her voice faded off. After several minutes of silence she continued, "And I don't know what I'm feeling. I'm just numb. It's a flashback to Iraq. I've walled myself in an emotional bunker."

After several minutes she asked, "I killed someone, didn't I?"

"You shot someone, fired in self defense. They may have died in the ensuing events. I didn't see any of it. What happened?"

Hannah's answer was slow in coming. "By the time we were back on the water, the wind had picked up and the boats were moving a lot with the waves coming off the lake and the rebounding water from the shelf ice. I was really worried about losing my hold on Tristan's boat. I was leaning over the back of his cockpit trying to keep our bows in line so we wouldn't be too difficult to tow. At first I didn't see anything. I just heard the pop. Then I glanced up at this dark form holding a pistol. I pulled out that little flare gun and took a wild shot. I can't believe I hit anything. And then there was the fire, the person toppling into the lake. It's all surreal... a dream... a nightmare. It's not like I haven't been around violence and death. But I've never...."

"The flare didn't inflict a mortal wound."

"But the fire. I started the chain of..."

"No, you just responded. You were protecting your patient. You were doing the only thing that could be done in that situation."

"Have you ever...?" Hanna left the opening of her question hang.

"Yes, similar situation. I was badly wounded, barely conscious of my actions. It was a desperate act of self-defense. I had one shot at him with my rescue knife. My assailant wandered off and died a week or more later from an infection." Ray paused and reflected on the incident that had taken place only a few months before. "That was a very difficult time. I'm still dealing with the psychological fallout, probably always will be. But before now, I never thought about the part I played in that young man's death. There was no other choice."

They rode in silence the rest of the way. On reaching the house, Simone came dashing out the instant Ray pushed the front door open. After absorbing her enthusiastic greeting of barks and wags and wet kisses as they passed her back and forth, they walked down his drive and then continued through the near neighborhood. The wind had dropped and the temperature was mild for early March. They strolled under streetlights and along the quiet streets of the village, both aware of the special gift of sharing tranquil moments with a friend and a dog.

49

Simone's sharp bark pulled Ray's attention from the nearly completed *Incident Report* he had been working on since arriving at the office. He had made an early morning stop at the hospital's morgue to ID Elise Lovell's body, his mood shaken by the lifeless visage of the once vibrant woman that he remembered so clearly from his brief encounters.

Sue settled in a chair near him, Simone wiggling excitedly in her arms.

"How are you?" he asked.

"Tired. Plane was real late. They told us weather-related, but it was a clear, beautiful flight. I wasn't on the ground until after midnight. Close to 2:00 when I finally made it to bed. I didn't figure you'd be too pleased having me stop by to pick her up at that hour. How was my girl? A good guest?"

Ray smiled.

"You look a bit worse for wear," observed Sue. "Anything happen in my absence?"

Ray added a few more words to the *Incident Report* and hit the print command. He retrieved the hardcopy from the tray and handed it to her. "Here's something to read while I get some coffee. Want some?"

"Sure," she responded, grasping the pages in her right hand.

When Ray returned to the room, Sue was sitting at the conference table, the pages of the report laid out in front of her. Ray set two clean mugs, a carafe of coffee, and a can of Diet Coke on the table.

She took the Coke, popped the opener, and looked over at Ray. "My God," slipped from her lips, her eyes returning to the print.

They sat in silence until she had completed the last page. When her eyes met his, Ray asked, "What did you learn yesterday? Help me understand how this all happened."

Sue retrieved a laptop from her backpack. "I started pulling notes together last night at O'Hare while I was waiting for the flight. It's just a rough draft, more of an outline, really." She looked over at Ray then back at the screen, as she opened a document. "Nice town, about ten or twelve thousand. Flat country out there. I met with Detective Sergeant Jeanette Walters; she looks like she's in her late 40s. Once I showed my identification and proved to her that I was who I said I was, she was very cordial. She's a real character."

"How so?" probed Ray.

"She was the first woman in the department and the first one with a college degree. She said she had a lot of challenges early on, she didn't elaborate. She just seemed to assume that I would understand.

"We walked from the public safety building to the library, just a couple of blocks. Along the way she explained that all the records on Elise had been sealed by order of the court. Elise was a juvenile at the time. When we got to the library, she introduced me to the research librarian, a Robert Kampy—tall, skeletal, smelling of pipe tobacco. I would guess that he's in his late 60s. It soon became apparent that Jeanette had prepared Robert for my visit. He took me in a back room and, behind closed doors, he led me through a series of microfilms from the local paper, a publication that no longer exists. There were reports of vandalism and arson, with the suggestion that teens were suspected."

"What are we taking about?" asked Ray.

"The surrounding country there is quite rural. The early articles referred to vacant houses being vandalized, interiors being badly damaged. The things left at the scenes, beer cans, lots of car tracks suggested the places had been the sites for a large party, probably by teens.

Then there were several articles on vacant homes being destroyed by fire, with the suggestion these were probably related to the earlier vandalism and that this was a very dangerous development. The last article he showed me was about a high school senior being killed in a fiery accident early on a Sunday morning. The boy who was killed was hit from behind while sitting at a stop sign. He was hit by a large dump truck, his gas tank exploded, and he died in the fire. Other than noting that the driver of the other vehicle was a minor, there was no identification."

"So what's all that about?"

"That's what I asked Kampy. He said the person at the wheel of the truck was Elise Brickston. The boy driving the car had been her steady. While Jeanette Walters had done her best to be a bit elusive, Kampy was not. He told me that she was the daughter of one of the wealthy members of the community. Her father had made millions running a large road-building company. He said that Elise was willful and wild and that the accident was no accident, it was murder with premeditation committed by a minor."

"So what happened?" asked Ray.

"That was his point, nothing happened. Elise was whisked out of town to some expensive treatment facility to help her recover from the horrible trauma of the accident and her overwhelming feelings of guilt and remorse.

"Kampy was bitingly sarcastic. He said he thought that Elise was probably pregnant and her parents wanted to get her out of town and get things taken care of. She was never charged. She was later sent to a pricy prep school, he said he heard it was in suburban Chicago. Kampy told me that some of the kids from town ran into Elise in college. She went to Northern Illinois. And he said he always wondered what might lay in her future. As far as he was concerned, she was a killer."

"So how does Kampy fit into this whole story?" asked Ray.

"It was his son, Eric, the boy who was killed in the accident. Kampy said that at that time he had figured out that his son was involved in the spree of vandalism and arson. He had confronted Eric just hours before he died. Eric had confessed to Kampy his involvement, but he told his father that Elise was at the center of it all. It was her idea, and he was going to break up with Elise because he was afraid that she would ruin his life. The night of the accident he was going out to meet her, to tell her that the relationship was over. Kampy isn't sure what happened, the order of events. But he is sure that his son was murdered and that Elise got away with it."

They sat in silence for several minutes. "That's a really good piece of work on your part. Reaching back twenty years, making the connections."

"Yes, it is," she agreed. "But after the fact, too late to protect anyone or bring Elise to justice. We end with questions rather than answers."

50

Ray and Sue did not have long to contemplate Sue's last remark. Their attention was pulled to a voice at the open door asking if she could come in. They turned to find Molly Birchard, looking tired and disheveled, standing just outside the doorway in the hall.

Ray came to his feet and escorted her into his office, shutting the door behind her. When she was seated at the conference table, he retrieved a digital recorder from his desk, turned it on, pressed the record function, and set it on the table between Sue, Molly, and himself.

"Where've you been?" he asked.

"I was staying with a friend. She lives outside Mt. Pleasant. It's a rural area. I thought it would be safe there. But after a couple of days I knew I had to come back, come home. As soon as I got to my mother's, she insisted that I come here. In fact, she drove me."

Molly sat in silence for several minutes, head down, staring at the desk in front of her. Finally Ray asked, "You have something you want to tell us?"

"Yes," she answered. "I just don't know where to begin."

"Begin at the beginning. Sue and I will ask you questions along the way to help us get your whole story," counseled Ray.

"There's just so much stuff," said Molly. "It's difficult. It's embarrassing. Some of it has to do with things about me that I've never told anyone. Maybe that I don't even want to admit to myself."

"You need to tell us everything," said Sue. "You've never done that. You've always just skirted along the surface. We need to hear it all. That's the only way we can help you." Sue's voice was low and soothing. Her eyes were locked on Molly's. "Understand?"

"Yes," Molly responded. She went silent again as she considered where to start. "Well, there is a history and then there is what happened in the last few weeks. And a lot of it is about me, things that I'm not comfortable with. Things I can't imagine telling anyone else.

"You know Brenda and me and Tristan go back a long way, back to Leiston School starting when we were in the tenth grade. It has to do with sex and drugs, and the three of us, and sometimes Richard Kinver, who was providing the grass in exchange for sex. There was another person, too."

"Who was that?" asked Sue.

"It was Elise. She was only at Leiston our senior year. And we didn't let her in the group until sometime in the winter. She was wilder than the rest of us. I didn't know what "kinky" was until I met Elise. Our little gatherings went on right through graduation and then we went off to college.

"Eventually Brenda and I found our way back up here and our friendship resumed. And then Tristan came back too. He was totally wigged out by then. As I think I told you, his brain had been scrambled in a climbing accident, and Brenda and I became sort of his keepers, Brenda more than me. She had really good organizational skills, knew how to look after him." Her voice dropped, "Sometimes I can barely look after myself.

"And then Elise was back in the area, too. Grown-up and sophisticated, the picture of a perfect mother and wife. And life went on. We were fairly normal functioning adults and what had happened at Leiston was a distant memory. And then everything changed and our world started to spin out of control."

"When was that?" probed Ray.

"It all started last spring or summer. Rod Gunne came into the picture and everything changed. It seemed innocent enough in the beginning. Here was this handsome guy with a lot of money who was giving Brenda, and indirectly, Elise a lot of work. And Brenda had been really

struggling. Along with everyone else, this has been a hard time for artists."

"Molly, you said things began to spin out of control," said Sue.
"Would you explain that?"

Molly rocked back and forth and then started, "It was this fall. Rod
was having a party at his house to celebrate the installation of Brenda's
work. There was some wonderful food and lots of good champagne."
Molly stopped.

"What else?" probed Sue.

"There was some dope, too. Some grass and some coke. I didn't
touch any of that. It's not my high."

"Who was there?"

"It was Brenda and me, Rod and Richard, Elise was there, too."

"How was Richard involved?" Ray asked.

"Richard had arranged the rental of the house to Rod. He looked
after the place for this elderly couple. They were snowbirds. Usually
they would drive to Arizona in this big old RV of some kind, but this
year they couldn't get it running. Richard helped them find another
vehicle, and he drove them out to Arizona. He'd been doing some work
for Rod at the church. Rod told him that he needed a place to live, that
he would probably build a house in the spring. So Richard showed him
that place. He charged Rod plenty of rent. Richard has been desperate
for money."

"Take us back to the party," said Sue.

"Like I was saying, a lot of champagne had been consumed. There is
this bumped out wall on the lakeside of the house with a big hot tub. We
all ended up in there. It was like we were 18 again, all hormones and no
brains. And that became a regular kind of thing, several times a week.
Rod started referring to us as *the ladies of the altar guild*.

"And then one evening Rod showed up with a video camera. And
the next time we got together he had a big screen next to the hot tub so
we could have instant replays. Things were becoming increasingly wild
and kinky. Brenda, who'd been holding back, really seemed to get into
it. She would take the recordings back home and produce them into a
video with a hard rock soundtrack and lots of breathing and moaning.
It was the wildest stuff I'd ever seen.

"One night we took the video over to the church, it was probably around two in the morning. Rod put it on all the screens and really cranked the audio. We drank more champagne and, well…" her voice trailed off.

"I could go on and on, but let me tell you what I think was going down. I think that Brenda had really fallen for Rod Gunne. And I think the same kind of thing was going on with Elise as well. And I think that Rod was more drawn to Elise than Brenda. Neither of them ever told me that, I could just see it. And by this time Brenda had tons of video. She could destroy him. He knew it. And then she was killed."

"Why didn't you tell us this before?" asked Sue.

"I couldn't do it. I was afraid. I was too involved. And I didn't know if Richard was involved, the truck and all. I was trying to protect him. But after he was killed, I assumed I was next. Rod Gunne, he's the killer. And I don't know about Elise, she's probably involved, too. But you've got to protect me, and my son and my mother."

Ray let her comment hang a long time before responding. "A lot has happened in the last few days. I don't think you're in danger anymore."

Molly sat there staring at Ray, looking like she expected to hear more.

"I can't really tell you anymore at the moment," he explained. "It will be on the news in the next few days. I want you to go to your mother's home and stay there. You are no longer in any danger. But I want you to be available in case we have any more questions. No trips outside the area and do not have any contact with Rod Gunne, understand?"

"Yes," she responded. "Am I in trouble with the law?"

"Probably not," Ray responded, "But I'm counting on your continued honesty and cooperation. You understand that?"

"Yes." Then she asked sheepishly, "Do you think I might be able to keep my job?"

"That's an issue that you will have to take up with the Human Resources Department. You disappeared without letting anyone know you weren't going to be showing up for work."

"Am I free to go now?" she asked, sensing that the conversation was at an end.

"Yes," said Ray, standing and escorting her to the door. He closed the door again and collapsed into his chair.

Looking at Sue he said, "It's a good thing that you are so skilled at details. There are a million loose ends here."

"And how do we explain all of this to the prosecutor?"

"How do we explain any of it to the prosecutor? It's part Greek tragedy, part soap opera, and probably no one is going to trial."

"How about Rod Gunne?" Sue asked.

"We've got to bring him in and interrogate him thoroughly. The polygraph results strongly suggest that he wasn't involved in any of the crimes, but we've got to squeeze him hard and break him down. And we've got enough information now to do it."

"Richard Kinver and Tristan" said Sue, "why did she want them dead?"

"There are some things we'll never really understand. In her warped view of the world they must have posed some kind of threat. I wonder where she thought it was all going to end. She didn't have parents to bail her out this time."

They sat for many minutes in complete silence. Finally Ray asked, "What are you thinking?"

"Two things. I'm trying to comprehend this whole situation, and I'm thinking a big cheeseburger medium rare with some real cheddar, some sweet potato fries, and a chocolate shake. How about you?"

"I'm with you on the first. But on the second, I'm thinking about pastrami on really good rye. I'm thinking Zingerman's."

"Ray, that's four hours away on bad roads."

"I'll take a laptop, and we will have hours of uninterrupted time where we can try to work through this whole case. And I'll buy."

"I'll drive." Sue looked over at Simone who was curled up on the one overstuffed chair in the office. "Come on girl," she said, "We're going on a road trip."

Author's Note: It Takes a Village

With *Shelf Ice* and all of my other books, I've been fortunate to have assistance and continued encouragement from so many friends and readers. Special thanks to the early readers of this manuscript, Diane Carr, Danny Carr, Anne-Marie Oomen, Heather Shaw, and Sandy Seppala. Their feedback was essential in shaping the story and eliminating the most egregious illiteracies. At the end Barbara Paton's careful proofing was critical in removing my many typos and omissions.

I am greatly indebted to Heather Shaw for the cover design and interior layout. I am in awe of her artistic skills and literary sensibilities.

And, finally, Mary K, who provides support, friendship, and wise counsel as the book moves from a few random notes to a final draft.